Alzheimer's Disease

Jacqueline Adams

LUCENT BOOKS
A part of Gale, Cengage Learning

Detroit • New York • San Francisco • New Haven, Conn • Waterville, Maine • London

Author Acknowledgements

I am indebted to Dr. William Klunk and Dr. Oscar Lopez of the University of Pittsburgh Alzheimer Disease Research Center for patiently answering my many questions. I would also like to thank John Pohlod for generously sharing his family's experience.

For their support and assistance, without which I would have been unable to complete this project, this book is dedicated to my parents, James and Doris Letera, and my parents-in-law, Donald and Janet Adams.

LIBRARY OF CONGRESS CATALOGING-IN-PUBLICATION DATA

Adams, Jacqueline, 1969-
  Alzheimer's disease / by Jacqueline Adams.
  p. cm. -- (Diseases & disorders)
  Includes bibliographical references and index.
  ISBN 978-1-4205-0553-5 (hardcover)
  1. Alzheimer's disease--Popular works. I. Title.
  RC523.2.A33 2011
  616.8'31--dc22

                                                      2010050809

Lucent Books
27500 Drake Rd.
Farmington Hills, MI 48331

ISBN-13: 978-1-4205-0553-5
ISBN-10: 1-4205-0553-X

Printed in the United States of America
1 2 3 4 5 6 7 15 14 13 12 11
Printed by Bang Printing, Brainerd, MN, 1st Ptg., 04/2011

Table of Contents

"The Most Difficult Puzzles Ever Devised"

Charles Best, one of the pioneers in the search for a cure for diabetes, once explained what it is about medical research that intrigued him so. "It's not just the gratification of knowing one is helping people," he confided, "although that probably is a more heroic and selfless motivation. Those feelings may enter in, but truly, what I find best is the feeling of going toe to toe with nature, of trying to solve the most difficult puzzles ever devised. The answers are there somewhere, those keys that will solve the puzzle and make the patient well. But how will those keys be found?"

Since the dawn of civilization, nothing has so puzzled people—and often frightened them, as well—as the onset of illness in a body or mind that had seemed healthy before. A seizure, the inability of a heart to pump, the sudden deterioration of muscle tone in a small child—being unable to reverse such conditions or even to understand why they occur was unspeakably frustrating to healers. Even before there were names for such conditions, even before they were understood at all, each was a reminder of how complex the human body was, and how vulnerable.

While our grappling with understanding diseases has been frustrating at times, it has also provided some of humankind's most heroic accomplishments. Alexander Fleming's accidental discovery in 1928 of a mold that could be turned into penicillin has resulted in the saving of untold millions of lives. The isolation of the enzyme insulin has reversed what was once a death sentence for anyone with diabetes. There have been great strides in combating conditions for which there is not yet a cure, too. Medicines can help AIDS patients live longer, diagnostic tools such as mammography and ultrasounds can help doctors find tumors while they are treatable, and laser surgery techniques have made the most intricate, minute operations routine.

This "toe-to-toe" competition with diseases and disorders is even more remarkable when seen in a historical continuum. An astonishing amount of progress has been made in a very short time. Just two hundred years ago, the existence of germs as a cause of some diseases was unknown. In fact, it was less than 150 years ago that a British surgeon named Joseph Lister had difficulty persuading his fellow doctors that washing their hands before delivering a baby might increase the chances of a healthy delivery (especially if they had just attended to a diseased patient)!

Each book in Lucent's Diseases and Disorders series explores a disease or disorder and the knowledge that has been accumulated (or discarded) by doctors through the years. Each book also examines the tools used for pinpointing a diagnosis, as well as the various means that are used to treat or cure a disease. Finally, new ideas are presented—techniques or medicines that may be on the horizon.

Frustration and disappointment are still part of medicine, for not every disease or condition can be cured or prevented. But the limitations of knowledge are being pushed outward constantly; the "most difficult puzzles ever devised" are finding challengers every day.

Replacing Myths with Knowledge

After supper, John drove up the road to check on his father. He found the elderly man sitting at the empty kitchen table. "Dad, did you eat?" John asked.

His father's shoulders sagged. "I don't have anything to eat."

"What do you mean, you don't have anything to eat?" John said. "Dad, your freezer is full."

"Oh, it is?"[1]

John sighed and opened the freezer. He helped his father pick out something for supper again.

This was a good day. At least John's father recognized him. On other days, he stares at John as if he is a stranger.

For thirty-five years, John's father was a respected school-teacher. He also sold tractors and could answer questions from memory about any tractor engine from any year. "The man had a mind like an encyclopedia," John said. "He was a smart man. And it's just gone."[2]

When John's father began showing symptoms of memory loss, his family thought it was simply forgetfulness that goes along with normal aging. As the symptoms worsened, they realized the situation was more serious. At age eighty, he was diagnosed with Alzheimer's disease (AD), an irreversible, incurable disease that gradually destroys brain tissue and robs people of their memory and thinking abilities.

John's father and other family members were ready to seek help when they became aware of the problem, but that is not always the case. AD is such a dreaded disease that sufferers often try to hide their symptoms out of embarrassment or fear of a diagnosis that will confirm the worst. Family members may be in denial, refusing to admit that something is wrong. At times, one close family member battles to convince others that a problem exists and that their loved one needs to see a doctor. Because people with AD may forget things one day and remember them the next, others sometimes mistakenly believe that they are faking the memory loss.

For many years, people thought that the symptoms of AD were a normal part of aging. Despite scientific breakthroughs of the past several decades, myths about AD persist. Many people refer to AD as "old-timer's" disease or think that all older people with memory problems have AD. Although AD is the most common cause of memory loss in the elderly, a hundred other causes exist. Another common belief is that only elderly people develop AD. The risk for AD does increase with age, but a rare form of AD strikes people in their thirties, forties, and fifties.

Other myths are that a diagnosis of AD means that a person's life is over and that people with AD are not aware of what goes on around them. Many people with AD live meaningful lives, using their time in the early stages of the disease to care for matters that are important to them. The effects of the disease on a person's thinking abilities vary with the individual and with time, but people with AD may still understand what is happening, and they appreciate being treated with respect.

Knowledge about AD helps family members not only to show respect but also to deal with their own pain. When his father fails to recognize him, John reminds himself that the disease is to blame. The children in the family are aware of the problem and do their best to interact with their grandfather. John said, "We just can talk to him the way we always

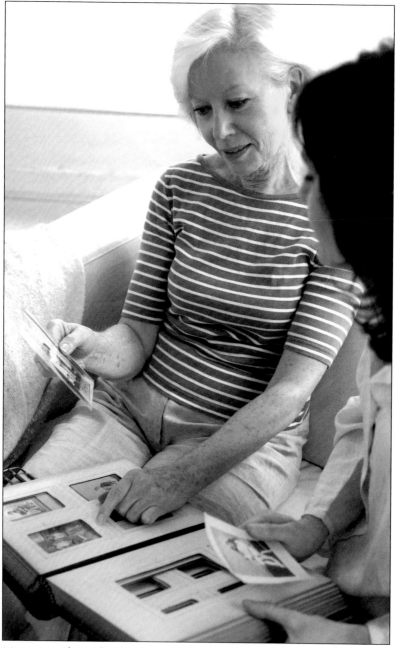

Many people with Alzheimer's disease live meaningful lives, using their time in the early stages of the disease to care for matters that are important to them.

talked to him. We might not get the same answer, or what we expect."[3]

With their ongoing search for knowledge about AD, scientists hope to do more than dispel myths and misunderstandings. Many studies are targeting ways to identify people who are at risk for the disease and to diagnose sufferers earlier. Researchers are working to gain insight into the causes of AD. They hope this will allow them to develop effective ways not only to treat AD but also to prevent it from developing at all.

CHAPTER ONE

Exposing an Enemy of Memory

For many years, people thought that the memory problems and other symptoms of Alzheimer's disease (AD) were the results of normal aging. Even after the disease was discovered and named, doctors believed it was a rare condition. Today, AD is well-known as the most common cause of memory loss in the elderly.

AD is a neurodegenerative disease—it causes loss of the brain's tissue over time. It begins by destroying brain cells, or neurons, in parts of the brain involved with recent memory. As the disease progresses, the damage spreads to other brain areas. As a result, memory and other cognitive abilities (thinking skills) are gradually lost.

Not Just Normal Aging

As people age, they often become somewhat forgetful but can still function normally in their daily lives. They may take longer to remember something, or they may rely more on calendars or notes, but they can still handle daily tasks, and they do not behave in inappropriate ways.

With AD, the situation is different. The symptoms go far beyond the forgetfulness that often goes along with aging. Memory loss becomes so severe that it interferes with daily living. Other cognitive abilities, such as use of language, math, and the ability to recognize familiar objects and people, are gradually lost. AD also alters a person's behavior and ability to perform everyday tasks. "Alzheimer's Disease is a condition that affects the whole way someone is," says James Galvin, a neurology and psychiatry professor at New York University's Langone Medical Center. "It affects their personality. It affects their behavior. It affects their thinking. It affects their memory. It affects their ability to speak."[4]

An MRI scan of a sixty-five-year-old patient with Alzheimer's. The disease has caused atrophy in the upper right and left areas (brown) and the ventricles (purple) have dilated from their normal size.

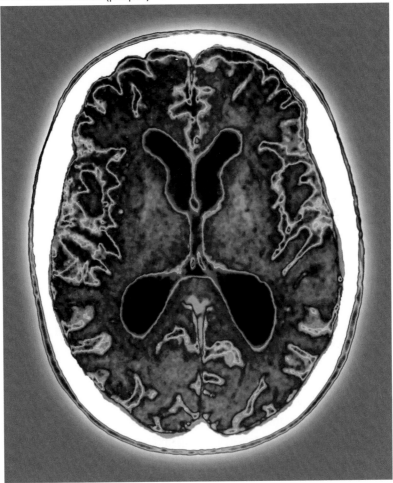

Warning Signs of Alzheimer's Disease

- Forgetting recent events and conversations, important dates, and facts recently learned
- Repeating themselves or asking the same question over and over
- Getting lost; not knowing where or when they are
- Problems with language, such as using the wrong words for items or stopping in the middle of a sentence and being unable to finish
- Trouble with familiar tasks, such as driving or cooking
- Problems with tasks requiring planning and organization, such as paying bills, making a grocery list, or following a recipe
- Trouble with tasks involving math or numbers
- Losing items because of inability to remember where they placed items or used them last
- Difficulty judging distances
- Poor judgment, such as giving too much money to telemarketers, going alone into dangerous areas, failing to attend to personal hygiene
- Personality changes, such as becoming depressed, confused, impulsive, suspicious, or easily angered
- Withdrawal from social activities; loss of interest in activities they once enjoyed

Even though aging itself does not explain AD, the risk of developing AD does increase with age. Most cases of AD occur in people sixty-five years of age or older. This is sometimes called late-onset AD. After age sixty-five, the number of people with AD doubles with every five-year increase in age. Only 5 percent of AD patients have early-onset AD. It strikes people in their forties and fifties, and sometimes as early as their thirties.

People often confuse AD with other types of dementia—conditions in which the brain's ability to function is affected to the point that it interferes with daily life. Doctors have found over a hundred different causes of dementia, including other neurodegenerative diseases, infections, and vitamin deficiencies. A few are reversible; most are not. AD is the most common cause of dementia in the United States, responsible for 50–80 percent of cases. It is currently irreversible. Researchers believe that the damage begins decades before symptoms appear.

How the Disease Progresses

Once symptoms become noticeable, AD progresses in three stages: mild, or early stage; moderate; and severe, or late stage. In mild, or early-stage, AD, people have trouble remembering what happened recently, although older memories remain. Other problems arise, such as getting lost and taking longer to complete everyday activities. Sufferers also begin to slowly lose the ability to handle tasks that take planning and organization, such as making a grocery list or balancing a checkbook. Small mood and personality changes may appear.

In moderate AD, the earlier problems continue to worsen, and new problems appear. Now sufferers may not recognize people they know or be aware of where they are or what the date is. They can no longer learn new things, and activities with multiple steps, such as dressing, become difficult. Not everyone with AD experiences behavioral problems, but some common problems in this stage are wandering, restlessness, sleep trouble, and personality changes. A formerly mild person may become aggressive and threaten, hit, or accuse others. A formerly energetic person may seem uninterested and depressed. Impulsive behavior, delusions, and paranoia often arise. For instance, a person may believe that family members have stolen items that he or she has misplaced.

In the mild and moderate stages, symptoms can come and go. A person seems to improve and remember things one day and then forgets them the next. Because of this, misunderstandings sometimes arise. Family and friends may become frustrated and wonder if the person is faking the memory problems.

By the time the disease has progressed to severe, or late-stage, AD, the brain is damaged to the point that the person needs help to accomplish even the most basic tasks, such as sitting up or walking. Sufferers no longer remember family members or even themselves. They lose control of bladder and bowels and may remain in bed most of the time. Some also lose the ability to speak and can make only grunting or moaning noises. Because they have trouble swallowing, they may stop eating. They remain completely dependent upon others until the disease results in their death. This final stage usually lasts from one to three years. Depending on factors such as the person's age and physical health, it may extend longer. Most AD patients live for an average of seven to nine years after the disease is diagnosed, but some live twenty years or more.

In the late stages of AD the brain is damaged to the point where the person needs help to accomplish the most basic tasks.

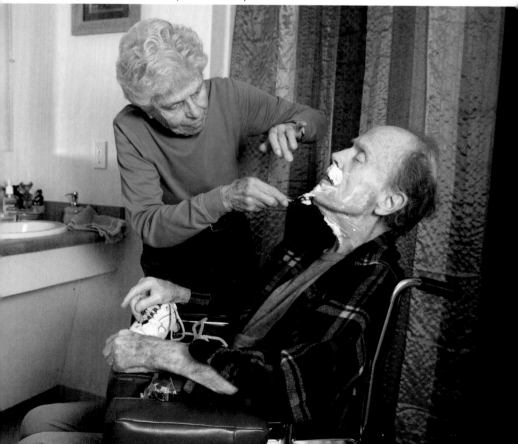

A Problem with a Long History

Although AD has become well-known as the cause of such devastating symptoms only in recent decades, ancient writers also described mental conditions that struck later in life. Most of them believed that the loss of mental abilities was a natural part of aging.

More than twenty-five hundred years ago, the Greek philosopher and mathematician Pythagoras stated that in old age, a person's mental abilities decline to the point that he returns to his infancy. Two centuries later, the Greek philosopher Aristotle wrote that in the elderly "there is not much left of the acumen of the mind which helped them in their youth, nor of the faculties which served the intellect, and which some call judgment, imagination, power of reasoning and memory."[5]

On the other hand, the Roman philosopher Cicero of the second century B.C. argued that the loss of mental abilities does not always accompany old age. He wrote that "senile debility, usually called dotage, madness or delirium, is a characteristic, not of all old men, but only those who are weak in will." He believed that people could prevent mental decline by keeping their minds active and stated that "it is our duty to resist old age; to compensate for its defects by a watchful care; to fight against it as we would fight against disease."[6]

In the second century A.D., the Roman physician Galen listed old age as one of the causes of a condition he called *morosis*. He described patients with this problem as "some in whom the knowledge of letters and other arts are totally obliterated; indeed they can't even remember their own names."[7]

Near the end of the eighteenth century, Scottish physician William Cullen classified loss of mental abilities in the elderly as a medical condition called *Amentia senilis*. He defined it as "imbecility of judgement, by which men either do not perceive the relation of things or forget them due to diminished perception and memory when oppressed with age."[8] Doctors later used the term *senile dementia* to refer to this condition.

An Unusual Case

Because doctors associated dementia with old age, a case that arose near the turn of the twentieth century puzzled them. In 1901, German neurologist and psychiatrist Alois Alzheimer began treating a woman with severe dementia symptoms. He referred to her in his notes as Auguste D. Because she was only fifty-one years old—much younger than most senile dementia patients—doctors believed her illness must have a different cause.

In his notes, Alzheimer described his work with the patient:

> *Writing* . . . When she has to write Mrs Auguste D., she writes Mrs and we must repeat the other words because she forgets them. The patient is not able to progress in writing and repeats, *I have lost myself.*

> *Reading*, she passes from one line to the next and repeats the same line three times. But, she correctly reads the letters. She seems not to understand what she reads. She stresses the words in an unusual way. Suddenly she says *twins. I know Mr Twin.* She repeats the word *twin* during the whole interview.

Her symptoms also included hallucinations and unpredictable behavior. Alzheimer wrote:

> During physical examination she cooperates and is not anxious. She suddenly says *Just now a child called, is he there?* She hears him calling . . . , she knows Mrs Twin. When she was brought from the isolation room to the bed she became agitated, screamed, was non-cooperative; showed great fear and repeated *I will not be cut. I do not cut myself.*[9]

Auguste D.'s condition worsened over the following years. Before she died in 1906, she was completely bedridden, unable to speak, and dependent on the hospital's staff to feed her and keep her clean.

Under the Microscope

After Auguste D.'s death, Alzheimer examined her brain tissue to try to learn the cause of her illness. He observed atrophy

German psychiatrist and neurologist Alois Alzheimer identified
the disease that bears his name in 1906.

(shrinkage) of her brain, which resulted from the death of
many neurons. Other doctors had already observed brain atrophy in patients with senile dementia. When Alzheimer prepared slides of her brain tissue with a new type of stain that
allowed him to see the parts of neurons beneath a microscope,

he discovered two abnormal features that surprised him.

The first surprise was that threadlike parts of neurons known as fibrils had tangled together into bundles. As these abnormal structures, which doctors now call neurofibrillary tangles, had grown, the neurons had disintegrated and died. The other abnormal structures were plaques—clumps of a sticky substance, later identified as amyloid protein, that had built up between neurons. Together, neurofibrillary tangles and amyloid plaques were the hallmarks of what Alzheimer believed to be a newly identified disease.

An electron micrograph shows neurofibrillary tangles as the dark clusters in the lower left corner and lower right. Dr. Alzheimer first identified these structures and the amyloidal plaques that had built up between neurons as the probable cause of the disease.

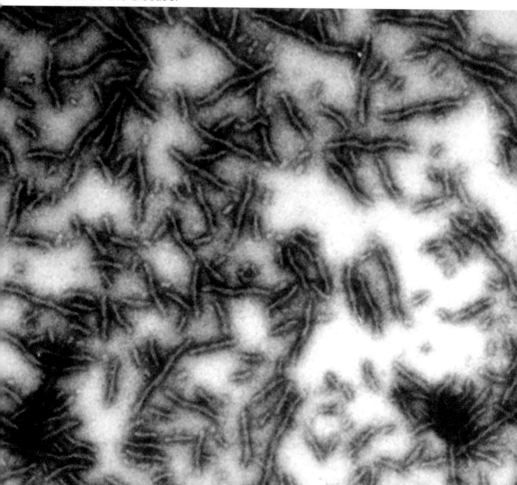

Doctors went on to identify other cases of people younger than sixty-five with the same symptoms and brain damage. In 1910, when psychiatrist Emil Kraepelin wrote a new edition of his *Textbook of Psychiatry*, he named the illness "Alzheimer's Disease." He wrote: "The clinical significance of this Alzheimer's Disease is still at the present time unclear. Although the anatomic findings would suggest the assumption that this is a matter of a particularly severe form of senile dementia, to some extent this is contradicted by the circumstance that the illness at times already begins at the end of the 40th year."[10] In other words, even though the symptoms looked like those of senile dementia, doctors thought that the patients were too young. They considered AD to be a separate condition, which they called pre-senile dementia.

In the following years, doctors examined brain tissue from hundreds of deceased patients who had suffered from similar symptoms. They found the same tangles and plaques in the brains of older people with senile dementia as they found in younger people who had been diagnosed with pre-senile dementia, or AD. Still, most doctors believed that senile dementia resulted from normal aging, so they thought that younger patients must have a separate disease.

Clearing Up the Confusion

The confusion continued for decades, with older patients being diagnosed with senile dementia and younger patients with the same symptoms being diagnosed with pre-senile dementia, or AD. Because cases of younger sufferers were rare, AD was considered a rare disease.

Doctors sometimes debated whether or not senile dementia and AD were the same disease, but very little research was performed. In the 1950s and 1960s, researchers used new technology—electron microscopes—to examine plaques and tangles. The differences they found between the brains of older people with and without senile dementia provided evidence that senile dementia does not result from normal aging. Rather, people with senile dementia were victims of disease—the same disease that sometimes struck younger people. Researchers came to realize that no matter how old or young the patients were, they all suffered from AD, which was not a rare disease after all.

Most people were unaware of the results of this research. Very little funding was set aside for studying AD, and the disease received little public attention. That began to change in 1976 when neurologist Robert Katzman wrote an editorial in the *Archives of Neurology*. From his research, Katzman realized that not only were AD and senile dementia the same illness but also that many people with AD had been misdiag-

Famous AD Sufferers Raise Awareness

During the late twentieth century when researchers were making strides in understanding AD, the plight of famous people helped raise public awareness of the disease. Hollywood actress Rita Hayworth appeared in movies from the 1930s until the early 1970s, when she could no longer remember her lines. Doctors misdiagnosed her for years before the public announcement in 1981 that she had AD. Her daughter cared for her until Hayworth's death in 1987 and became active in raising funds to fight the disease.

Former U.S. president Ronald Reagan died in 2004 after a long battle with AD. Nearly ten years earlier, he wrote a letter to inform the American people of his diagnosis. In the letter, he explained why he and his wife had decided to reveal his condition. He wrote:

"In the past Nancy suffered from breast cancer and I had my cancer surgeries. We found through our open disclosures we were able to raise public awareness. We were happy that as a result many more people underwent test-

nosed with other types of dementia. He estimated that AD was the fourth or fifth leading cause of death in the United States. He added:

> The argument that Alzheimer disease is a major killer rests on the assumption that Alzheimer disease and senile dementia are a single process and should, therefore, be considered a single disease. Both Alzheimer disease and senile dementia are progressive dementias with similar changes in mental and neurological status that are indistinguishable by careful clinical analyses.[11]

ing. They were treated in the early stages and able to return to normal, healthy lives.

"So now, we feel it is important to share it with you. In opening our hearts, we hope this might promote greater awareness of this condition. Perhaps it will encourage a clearer understanding of the individuals and families who are affected by it."

Ronald Reagan. Letter to the American People. November 5, 1994. www.alz.co.uk/media/reaganletter.html.

Former president Ronald Reagan and his wife, Nancy, pose for pictures at Reagan's first public appearance after he announced he was diagnosed with Alzheimer's disease. Reagan is credited with raising public awareness of the disease.

A Turning Point

As awareness about AD grew, so did funding for research. In the early 1980s Katzman helped found the organization that later became known as the Alzheimer's Association, which provides private funding for research, support for people with AD and their families, and public education about the disease. In the United States, Congress began setting aside more funds for Alzheimer's research through the National Institute on Aging (NIA). T. Franklin Williams, who served as the director of the NIA from 1983 to1991, stated that "we had come to recognize that Alzheimer's dementia was probably the greatest scourge and disaster for older people and their families in the United States, and as well the growing potential in our scientific community to address its challenges. We made Alzheimer's research our highest priority."[12]

During this time, researchers gained insight into the formation of amyloid plaques and neurofibrillary tangles and developed new techniques for studying AD. In 1998, neurologist François Boller and speech and language pathologist Margaret M. Forbes wrote in a medical article: "This improved understanding has led to a completely new attitude toward dementia which is no longer considered an unavoidable part of aging. Alzheimer's disease has become a 'household' word and it is not unusual to hear families of AD subjects as well as patients with diagnosis of AD discuss freely the condition with relatives or even with strangers."[13]

Scope of the Problem

According to a 2010 Alzheimer's Association report, AD was the seventh leading cause of death in the United States that year, and every seventy seconds, someone developed the disease. An estimated 5.3 million Americans had AD in 2010, including 5.1 million who were older than age sixty-five and 200,000 with the rarer, early-onset form of the disease. More women have AD than men, but researchers believe this simply reflects the fact that women, on average, live longer than men

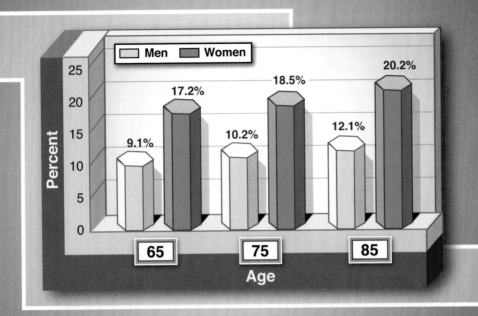

Estimated Lifetime Risks for Alzheimer's by Age and Sex

Men   Women

Percent

25
20
15
10
5
0

9.1%
17.2%
10.2%
18.5%
12.1%
20.2%

65   75   85

Age

Taken from: Alzheimer's Association. *2010 Alzheimer's Disease Fact and Figures Report.*

do. There is no significant difference between the number of women and men of the same age who have AD.

The number of AD sufferers is expected to multiply over the next few decades. Advances in medical treatment and improvements in living conditions mean that people are living longer. Today, 5.5 million Americans are age eighty-five or older. By 2050, that number is expected to rise to 19 million. Since the risk of developing AD increases with age, cases of AD will rise as the population ages. Experts estimate that by 2050, between 11 and 16 million Americans will have AD if no cure, effective treatment, or prevention has been found.

The Toll on Others

Besides AD patients, millions of other people are affected by the disease. In 2009, an estimated 10.9 million people served as unpaid caregivers for someone with AD or another dementia. Ninety-four percent of the caregivers were family members, and the rest were friends. Each caregiver spent an average of 21.9 hours per week tending to the needs of a dementia patient. This added up to 12.5 billion hours of unpaid caregiving in a single year.

The disease also takes an economic toll. The costs of health care and long-term care for people with AD and other dementias were expected to total $172 billion in 2010. Besides the direct costs, AD causes money to be lost in other ways. A 2002 study showed that United States businesses lost $36.5 billion that year because employees missed work or quit and had to be replaced so that they could care for someone with AD. No figures exist to measure the emotional and mental costs for AD patients and their loved ones.

Despite growing awareness of the problem and its scope, most sufferers do not receive a diagnosis until the disease is already in the moderate stage. Accurate methods of diagnosis are available, and early diagnosis carries many benefits for patients and their families.

CHAPTER TWO

Diagnosing Alzheimer's Disease

Alzheimer's disease is the most common cause of dementia, but a hundred different causes exist. During the decades when AD was poorly understood, telling the difference between it and other conditions was a challenge. Doctors had to examine the patient's brain tissue after death in order to diagnose AD. Today, an autopsy is still the only method of diagnosing AD with 100 percent certainty, but researchers have developed tools and methods that allow diagnosis with great accuracy in living patients.

Even though an early diagnosis is easily available from experienced doctors, most people with AD are not diagnosed until the disease has already reached the moderate stage. Some sufferers neglect to seek a diagnosis because they expect to experience some forgetfulness as they grow older. "Usually, the early signs and symptoms are interpreted as normal aging,"[14] says neurologist Oscar Lopez, director of the University of Pittsburgh Alzheimer Disease Research Center (ADRC). Only later, when the symptoms become worse, do they realize that a problem exists.

Others fear a diagnosis of a disease such as AD, which has no cure. They may hide their symptoms and resist going to a doctor, even after family members notice that something is wrong; however, an early diagnosis can benefit patients and their families.

Neurodegenerative Diseases
That Cause Dementia

A dementia evaluation allows doctors to determine the cause of the problem so that they can prescribe appropriate treatment. Because many other conditions have similar symptoms, these must be ruled out in order for a person to be diagnosed with AD. Some of the other conditions that cause dementia are also neurodegenerative diseases, which destroy brain cells over time.

The second most common cause of dementia is vascular dementia, a neurodegenerative disease caused by decreased blood flow to the brain. This can happen when a blood vessel that brings oxygen to the brain either bursts or is blocked by a blood clot, resulting in a stroke. Besides a stroke or a series of strokes, high blood pressure, atherosclerosis (hardening and narrowing of arteries), or other conditions that affect blood flow may cause vascular dementia. The symptoms usually begin suddenly and worsen quickly, unlike the gradual onset and worsening of AD symptoms. Vascular dementia patients lose planning and organizational skills and have trouble with language and balance, but their memory problems may not be as severe as those of AD patients.

Abnormal protein deposits called Lewy bodies form inside neurons as part of another disease, known as dementia with Lewy bodies. People with this disease suffer from muscle stiffness, which causes a shuffling walk and stiff facial expression. Other symptoms include hallucinations, tremors, loss of coordination and thinking abilities, and memory problems.

People with Parkinson's disease also suffer from muscle stiffness and tremors caused by damage to the brain, but not all develop problems with thinking and memory. Twenty to 40 percent of patients with Parkinson's disease do go on to develop Parkinson's disease dementia. Lewy bodies also play a role in this disease, and the symptoms are similar to those of dementia with Lewy bodies.

Other abnormal structures—Pick's bodies—form inside neurons in the class of diseases known as frontotemporal dementia. Unlike AD, in which damage begins in brain areas involved with recent memory, damage in these diseases begins in the brain's frontal lobes. Symptoms often appear at an earlier age than in AD patients, and thinking and behavior are affected before memory is. Problems with language—finding the right words, understanding the meaning of words, and repeating phrases over and over—get progressively worse. People with frontotemporal dementia may lose inhibitions and begin to act in ways that they normally would not. For example, they may begin swearing, shoplifting, or undressing in public.

Computer artwork of neurons (blue) with abnormal protein deposits called Lewy bodies (red) that are found in the brains of patients with Parkinson's disease dementia.

Other Causes of Dementia

Besides neurodegenerative diseases, many other conditions cause dementia. Nutritional dementia—also called Wernicke-Korsakoff syndrome, or alcohol dementia—results from a vitamin B1 (thiamine) deficiency. Since heavy drinking affects the body's ability to absorb vitamin B1, the most common cause of this syndrome is years of alcoholism. Other causes include malnourishment, crash diets, and kidney dialysis. Early on, problems with learning and memory may be even worse than with AD. Doctors treat the condition with vitamin B1 shots. When alcoholism is the cause, the dementia symptoms stop worsening and may improve if the person stops drinking early enough, but they may be irreversible if the problem continues longer.

Less common causes of dementia include other vitamin deficiencies, infections such as HIV and syphilis, and disorders of the thyroid, kidneys, or liver. When spinal fluid is blocked from flowing through the brain and spinal cord, it builds up in the brain in a condition known as normal pressure hydrocephalus. This causes dementia, changes in speech and the way a person walks, and incontinence of bladder and bowels. Damage stops if the condition is treated early on by inserting a shunt that allows spinal fluid to drain from the brain.

Many medications or combinations of medications can cause dementia symptoms, especially in people older than age sixty-five. The effects are reversed when they stop using the medications. Depression and other emotional problems are sometimes mistaken for dementia, since they affect a person's ability to concentrate. The effects of vision and hearing loss can also be misinterpreted as dementia. When these problems are addressed, the symptoms go away.

Seeking a Diagnosis

Because symptoms of AD and other dementias can seem similar, especially in the early stages, seeking a diagnosis from a doctor who is experienced with AD is important. In some cases, a primary care physician (PCP) diagnoses the patient

Screening Tests

Doctors often give patients a screening test to detect memory and thinking problems. One of the most common is the Mini-Mental State Exam (MME). In this short test, the doctor asks a patient simple questions such as what year it is and what state and town they are in. The patient is also asked to complete several tasks, such as counting backwards by sevens from 100, naming two objects that the doctor holds up, making up and writing a sentence, and copying a drawing of different shapes.

Another common test is clock drawing. The patient is instructed to draw a clock face and put numbers on it. Then the doctor asks the patient to make the clock read a certain time, such as ten minutes past eleven.

Researchers at the Ohio State University developed another screening tool called the SAGE test, a ten- to fifteen-minute test that doctors provide so patients can test themselves in the waiting room before an appointment. This tool can be downloaded from www.sagetest.osu.edu.

As part of the Mini-Mental State Exam to detect memory and thinking problems, a patient is given a "name the object" exercise.

and prescribes treatment. Because PCPs have to stay informed about a great many health problems that could affect their patients, not all of them are familiar with the latest information on AD. Patients are often referred to specialists such as neurologists, geriatricians, and psychiatrists for diagnosis. Clinics and research centers that specialize in dementia can provide a thorough evaluation.

In order for a person to be diagnosed with AD, his or her symptoms must match a list of criteria that experts have put together. The criteria listed in the *Diagnostic and Statistical Manual of Mental Disorders* (DSM), published by the American Psychiatric Association, are commonly used. They state that the patient must have developed multiple cognitive problems, which include memory loss, and disturbances in at least one other area. These areas are language, motor skills, the ability to recognize familiar objects or people, and planning and organizational skills.

The diagnostic criteria state that these problems must involve a significant loss from a level the patient experienced before. In other words, if one always had trouble remembering names, the fact that one forgets them now is not a sign of AD. The symptoms also begin gradually and continue to worsen, and doctors must rule out other causes.

The Dementia Evaluation

To determine whether the patient meets the diagnostic criteria for AD, health-care providers use a variety of tools. They speak with the patient and his or her family to learn about the symptoms, how daily functioning has changed, and the patient's medical history and overall health. Patients or their families may also fill out questionnaires. These usually include details about memory and thinking problems, changes in activity and behavior, and whether the patient is able to carry out everyday activities alone, with help, or not at all.

The evaluation includes neuropsychological testing—tests of different cognitive abilities, including memory, language, and problem solving. A physical examination and medical tests

As part of a three- to four-hour evaluation, patients are given a series of neuropsychological tests to evaluate a variety of cognitive functions, including visual-spatial function, executive function, and memory and language function.

help determine whether something else could be causing the dementia. For example, blood tests may reveal vitamin deficiencies or infections. Psychiatrist William Klunk, codirector of the University of Pittsburgh Alzheimer's Disease Research Center, summarizes what patients experience in a dementia evaluation at that facility:

> In a three- or four-hour evaluation, they get a series of neuropsychological tests that test a variety of different cognitive functions—memory, visual-spatial function, executive function, language function, all of these things. They're seen by a neurologist to see if they have other neurological symptoms that might be involved. They're seen by a psychiatrist to look for depression and other co-morbidities [additional, related medical problems]. Their basic physical health is evaluated to see if there's something that could be causing the memory impairment. After this evaluation, we look for a typical constellation of current symptoms and a typical history of development symptoms.[15]

Brain imaging—usually magnetic resonance imaging (MRI), which uses a magnetic field and sound waves to create a computerized image, or computed tomography (CT), which puts together many X-rays to form a cross-sectional image—is part of the evaluation. This could reveal damage that resulted from some other cause, such as vascular problems, or it could reveal the type of damage doctors would expect to see from AD. Klunk explains, "What we're typically looking for is the absence of tumors or strokes, and the presence of brain shrinkage in a specific pattern."[16] Doctors may repeat tests to see how the symptoms change over time.

Different Diagnoses

The information collected during the dementia evaluation helps doctors make a diagnosis. In research clinics, investigators use the terms *probable* and *possible AD*. *Possible AD* means that the dementia symptoms could be caused by AD, but they could also be caused by another problem that the evaluation has revealed. Lopez explains, "The term 'possible' is commonly used when the patient has some other illness that can also cause cognitive problems. For example, a person can have a stroke that affects his/her cognitive abilities, and Alzheimer's disease. Therefore, the word 'possible' indicates that the patient has two conditions that can affect cognition."[17] If no other cause is found, the diagnosis is probable AD. The diagnosis is worded that way because even though doctors can diagnose AD with 90 percent accuracy, they cannot give a definite diagnosis of AD without an autopsy. Outside of research clinics, doctors may not always distinguish between possible and probable AD.

Instead of AD, the diagnosis could be mild cognitive impairment (MCI). People with this condition have greater memory problems than are normal for their age but not as severe as the memory problems of people with dementia. For some people with MCI, the symptoms stay the same or even improve. For others, the problems progress until they develop AD or another dementia. People with MCI are at greater risk for developing AD than people without it.

Researchers still do not understand why some people with MCI develop AD and others do not. One hypothesis is that, for some patients, MCI may be a form of preclinical AD—a very early stage in which the symptoms have not yet progressed enough to allow doctors to diagnose the problem. For other patients, MCI may have other causes, such as depression, strokes, side effects of medication, or another illness. Klunk explains:

> I think the easiest way to think about mild cognitive impairment as it's currently defined is that a subset of people with mild cognitive impairment will go on to develop Alzheimer's disease. And those people probably really have the pathology of Alzheimer's disease present when they have mild cognitive impairment. It's just the mild end of the same spectrum. But some people who have clinically defined mild cognitive impairment don't have Alzheimer's disease and will never get Alzheimer's disease. They have mild cognitive impairment for other reasons.[18]

People who have mild cognitive impairment (MCI) have greater memory problems than are normal for their age, but not as severe as people with dementia. Some people improve; others develop AD or another dementia.

Benefits of an Early Diagnosis

Although a diagnosis is within reach, people with memory problems often hesitate to seek one. "It's a recurring problem," says neurologist Douglas Scharre of the Ohio State University Medical Center. "People don't come in early enough for a diagnosis, or families generally resist making the appointment because they don't want confirmation of their worst fears. Whatever the reason, it's unfortunate because the drugs we're using now work better the earlier they are started."[19]

An early diagnosis carries many benefits. It allows doctors to determine the true cause of the problem so they can address it properly. In a few cases, the cause turns out to be something that is reversible with proper treatment. In other cases, the condition may not reverse, but it will not get worse if the patient seeks treatment in time.

Even if the diagnosis is AD, treatment is most effective if it is started early. The drugs used to treat AD cannot reverse the damage or cure the disease, but they can help preserve the patient's mental functioning for months or years longer than would have been the case without them. The diagnosis can help prevent problems by putting family members on the alert at an early stage. For example, once family members know about the situation, they can remind the person with AD to take needed medications.

An early diagnosis also allows people with AD to make plans and be involved with decisions about the future while they are still able. They can plan where they will live when they can no longer care for themselves and how their financial matters will be handled. They may also decide to participate in research studies in order to help doctors understand the causes of AD and develop better treatments for the future.

Angela Lunde, a dementia education specialist at the Mayo Clinic's Alzheimer's Disease Research Center, writes:

> I feel strongly that persons are empowered when they receive an early diagnosis. They begin to understand that the changes and challenges are likely part of a disease

process—not a lack of effort, motivation, or sign of weakness. An early diagnosis offers the patient and their family time to arm themselves with knowledge and take full advantage of existing strengths. And early diagnosis allows for psychiatric symptoms such as depression to be identified and treated. I don't want to imply that an early diagnosis provides individuals and families with rose colored glasses (nobody wishes for the diagnosis

Reactions to the Diagnosis

People react to a diagnosis of AD in different ways. One member of an early-stage support group said, "This is a major attack on your confidence. You think 'This isn't fair! Why me?'"[1]

Others are relieved to finally know what the problem is. A woman diagnosed with AD in her late forties said, "It was a relief to me because there was a name to it. Although it is an incurable disease, at least I knew what I was dealing with."[2]

In a study published in 2008, Washington University researchers examined how a diagnosis of AD or mild cognitive impairment (MCI) affected rates of depression and anxiety in patients. They observed no significant changes in depression. In many cases, anxiety decreased after the diagnosis. The researchers concluded: "Disclosure of a dementia diagnosis does not prompt a catastrophic emotional reaction in most people, even those who are only mildly impaired, and may provide some relief once an explanation for symptoms is known and a treatment plan is developed."[3]

1. Quoted in National Institutes of Health. *What Happens Next?* August 2007, p. 6.
2. Alzheimer's Association. "Kris's Story." www.alz.org/living_with_alzheimers_ 8810.asp.
3. Medscape Today. "Reaction to a Dementia Diagnosis in Individuals with Alzheimer's Disease and Mild Cognitive Impairment," August 20, 2008. www.med scape.com/viewarticle/577972.

and the journey will not be easy), but instead it does help them with an understanding and a plan for whatever the future will bring.[20]

Family and friends who will serve as caregivers for the person with AD benefit from having time to learn about the disease. They can set up a support system in advance and learn ways to deal with upcoming difficulties. Many challenges arise from living with AD, both for patients and for caregivers.

CHAPTER THREE

Living with Alzheimer's Disease

The loss of memory and other thinking abilities means that people with AD can no longer carry out their daily activities in the way that they once did. As the disease progresses, they need more and more help to care for matters that they were used to handling on their own. Many people with AD also experience behavior and personality changes, which present additional challenges.

The challenges of living with AD affect not only people who have the disease, but also those close to them. As the disease progresses, caregivers must take on increasing responsibility in order to make sure that the person with AD is safe and his or her needs are being met. Caregivers must also find ways to manage problems that arise from behavior and personality changes in the person with AD.

Losing Independence

A big challenge for many people with AD is coming to terms with the idea of losing their independence. Mary Ann Becklenberg, who was diagnosed with AD at age sixty-two, says, "Prior to having this disease, I wasn't a person who needed to ask for help much. But now I do, and it's been a blow to my self-assurance and self-esteem. I can't participate fully in life like I used to, and it's a huge loss."[21]

Seventy percent of people with AD and other dementias live at home, where they receive help and care from family and friends. Others live in institutional settings, such as nursing homes or extended-care facilities. Studies show that around 94 percent of unpaid caregivers are relatives of the person with AD, while the others are friends.

The caregiver's role depends on the situation and needs of the person with AD. This role can change as the disease progresses. Besides making sure that the person with AD takes medications and pays bills at the right time, caregivers help with shopping, cooking, and transportation. They arrange for medical care, try to handle behavioral problems that arise, and keep the person with AD safe from danger. Eventually, they need to help the person with everyday tasks such as dressing, bathing, and using the toilet. Some caregivers take responsibility for the person twenty-four hours a day, seven days a week.

Studies have shown that around 94 percent of unpaid caregivers are relatives of the person with Alzheimer's.

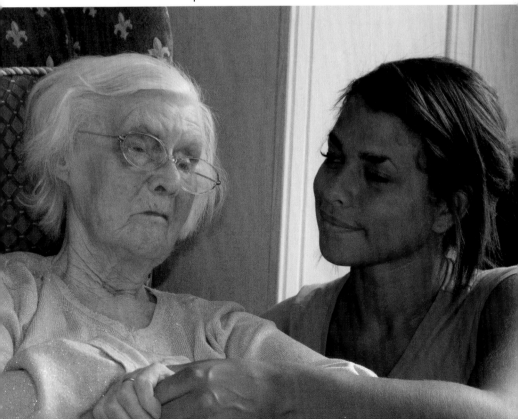

Coping with Memory Problems

As the mild forgetfulness of early AD progresses to more severe memory loss, this can create frustration for both the person with AD and for caregivers. People with AD often ask the same question over and over. They remember certain details but forget others, or they remember something today that they were unable to remember yesterday and will be unable to remember tomorrow. Because the disease strikes recent memory first, they may recall seemingly unimportant details from years ago but forget important information from the present. For example, they may forget current family members but remember the name of their first-grade teacher.

An Alzheimer's patient holds a special clock that gives the day of the week as well as the time. AD strikes recent memory first, making normal, everyday functions difficult.

Family and friends often feel hurt or distressed when their loved one fails to remember them. They may also feel frustrated at having to answer the same questions repeatedly. Experts recommend keeping in mind that these problems are caused by the disease and that AD sufferers cannot choose what or when they will remember.

Many caregivers report that keeping a sense of humor helps everyone to cope. Kathy Hatfield cofounded KnowItAlz, a web resource for caregivers, after she began caring for her father, who has AD. She shared this experience on her blog:

> Dad has the same breakfast every day. It consists of a bowl of bran cereal, a banana and a glass of orange juice. Yesterday, he got up, ate breakfast and headed to the shower. When he emerged from the bathroom, he asked me if he had already eaten, and I responded with a simple, "yes." He bowed his head and glumly replied, "I can't believe I can't remember eating breakfast. My mind must be *completely* gone." Dad was really sad and worried, so I said, "If you can't remember, you had Fillet Mignon, Eggs Benedict, sourdough toast with real butter and a big glass of champagne for breakfast." He laughed so hard, he forgot that he was frustrated. Laughter *is* the best therapy; for *both* of us![22]

Communication Difficulties

As memory and other thinking abilities decline, communication becomes more difficult. People with AD may start a sentence and forget what they were trying to say, or they may have trouble finding the right words. When others speak, AD sufferers may have trouble understanding the meaning of words or paying attention. These problems can frustrate the person with AD, who is struggling to be understood, and the caregivers, who are struggling to understand and to get their own points across. In the case of AD sufferers who spoke a different language as a child, the challenge can become even greater. Since AD first robs more recent memories while leaving old ones intact, these people may begin to speak and understand only their original language.

By being careful about the way they word sentences, caregivers may be able to improve communication. If they offer simple instructions, one step at a time, this may assist the person with AD to complete tasks. Since the person may have trouble understanding the meaning of words, repeating a thought in different words sometimes helps. Questions that can be answered with a yes or no or that offer only two choices are easier for someone with AD to answer. For example, in the guide *Caring for a Person with Alzheimer's Disease*, the National Institute on Aging suggests asking, "Are you tired?" instead of "How do you feel?" and "Would you like a hamburger or chicken for dinner?" instead of "What would you like for dinner?"[23]

Patiently allowing time for the person with AD to complete his thought helps communication and shows respect. Interrupting or speaking about the person to others as if the person were not there only adds to his or her frustration. Nonverbal communication, such as facial expressions, gestures, or a touch on the arm, can also help get ideas across.

Changes in Personality and Behavior

Besides problems with memory and communication, many different personality and behavioral changes can arise in a person who has AD. Not everyone with AD experiences these problems. Some may have a few mild problems or none at all. Others have catastrophic reactions. They become upset, and sometimes even aggressive, over matters that seem trivial to others.

Many different factors can prompt these changes. The damage to the brain that AD causes and the memory loss and confusion that go along with it can create feelings of anxiety, fear, or depression. These emotions can then trigger problem behaviors. Other factors, such as medications, illness, stress, and pain, can also have this effect. Figuring out what is behind the problem allows caregivers to address the cause and sometimes prevent the problem from happening again.

Agitation and Aggression

A common problem among people with AD is agitation—a state of being worried, disturbed, and restless. Some people

Common Behavior Problems of Alzheimer's Sufferers

- agitation
- pacing
- aggression
- sleep problems
- sundowning
- rummaging/hoarding
- wandering
- hallucinations
- delusions/paranoia
- forgetting to bathe or change clothes
- inappropriate behavior (undressing in public, shoplifting)

show their agitation by pacing back and forth. A change in routine, a new caregiver, or unfamiliar surroundings can create anxiety, fear, and confusion. These feelings, in turn, may trigger agitation. Pain, loneliness, lack of sleep, or other factors can be at the root of the problem. Agitation can also be a reaction to the losses that people with AD experience, such as the loss of a home, driver's license, or abilities that were important to them.

In some cases agitation leads to aggressive behavior. The person may shout at or even hit others. Experts agree that such problems usually have a cause, and addressing that cause may help stop the problem. Psychiatrist Stephen Soreff offers an example based on his experience with nursing home residents: "When a resident with dementia contracts an infection, he may have difficulty telling others of his discomfort, and an aggressive outburst may be his way of communicating it. Based on our work in many long-term care facilities, we have found that unexpressed and unrecognized pain can lead to aggressive events."[24]

Sleep Problems and Sundowning

Sleep problems are also common. The person may not want to go to bed or may have trouble sleeping through the night. This can add to the exhaustion of caregivers. Samara Howard, who quit her job to become a full-time caregiver for her mother, says, "Normally, I only sleep maybe two hours a night because she wakes up and she wanders and she turns on the stove."[25]

Sundowning, or increased agitation in the late afternoon or evening, can also disturb sleep patterns. Some experts think that the dimmer evening light may increase a person's confusion, and this could contribute to sundowning. They recommend keeping the person's surroundings well lit to address the problem. Other suggestions for dealing with sleep problems and sundowning are to keep the person active earlier in the day so he or she will be tired at bedtime, limiting caffeine, playing soft music in the evening, making sure the person's bed is comfortable, and keeping the same bedtime every night. Activities that take much effort, such as bathing, can be done early in the day so they do not create agitation in the evening.

Wandering

An estimated six out of ten people with AD will wander at some point. This can be dangerous for the person who wanders and terrifying for the caregivers. Often, people who wander are trying to return "home." They do not remember their current home and are looking for a place they lived decades earlier. Others are trying to go to work or to care for another responsibility that ended long ago. Since many have trouble communicating and may not even remember their names, they cannot ask for help when they get lost.

Even the most attentive caregiver will find it impossible to watch the person with AD every minute of the day and night. Installing a system that chimes when a door opens or installing locks higher or lower than normal, where the person with AD will not see them, can prevent wandering. Sometimes disguising the door with a curtain or placing a mirror on the door prevents people with AD from going outside.

Caregivers can take measures ahead of time to make sure that the person returns safely if he or she wanders. They can let neighbors and local police know about the problem so that everyone will be on the alert. An ID bracelet will ensure that anyone who finds the wanderer understands the problem and knows whom to call, even if the person with AD cannot communicate. Caregivers can also enroll the person in the Alzheimer's Association Safe Return program, which provides twenty-four-hour emergency help.

Rummaging and Hoarding

Some people with AD rummage through closets, drawers, cupboards, or the refrigerator. This sometimes results from boredom, or they may be searching for something that they cannot

Emergency personnel attend to an eighty-year-old woman found wandering a mile from her house. Often people who are wandering are trying to return home but cannot find their way.

name. They may also hoard items in different hiding places. This behavior is not always harmful, but it can create problems if the person hides needed or valuable items, especially if the items get put in the trash container. It can also be a safety issue if the person rummages through dangerous items or finds spoiled food in the back of the refrigerator and eats it. This behavior can put stress on caregivers as they constantly clean up the rummaged areas or search for missing items.

To keep the person safe, caregivers may need to lock away dangerous items and be quick to throw away spoiled food. If the person hides or throws away mail, renting a post office box is one way to solve the problem. Providing the person with his or her own place to rummage, such as a cupboard or a box of objects that interests him or her, can also help.

Hallucinations and Delusions

AD patients sometimes experience hallucinations—imagining that they see, hear, smell, feel, or taste something that is not real. The most common types of hallucinations involve sight and hearing. For example, the person may insist that he hears music or that he sees a long-dead relative present in the room. Hallucinations can be caused by AD or by other factors, such as medication or another illness.

If the hallucinations do not bother the person, caregivers may not need to do anything to address them. Telling the person that the hallucination is not real only leads to an argument. If the person is upset or frightened by the hallucinations, caregivers can offer reassuring words and/or another activity for a distraction. Doctors can prescribe antipsychotic medications as a last resort if the hallucinations cause severe distress.

Delusions, or false beliefs, can also create stress. This is especially true when the person with AD has paranoia, a type of delusion in which someone believes others are trying to hurt him or her. The person may believe that a family member is trying to poison him or that the caregiver is stealing her possessions. This sometimes happens when the person with AD puts his glasses or her purse somewhere and does not remember doing so.

Support Groups

For people who are diagnosed with AD soon enough, an early-stage support group may help them to cope. They meet with other people who have AD to share experiences, get information, and receive emotional support. One woman who took part in an early-stage support group said, "I have found it extremely positive to find out as much as I can about others who are affected." In some groups, caregivers also participate for part of the session.

Support groups also exist for caregivers. These can be especially helpful if caregivers choose one whose members are caring for people in the same stage of AD. Some are online groups, which is convenient for caregivers who have a hard time getting away from home.

Support group locations can be found through the following website: www.alz.org/apps/we_can_help/support_groups.asp. These also include groups for children and teenagers, people with early-onset AD, and other special needs.

Quoted in National Institutes of Health. *What Happens Next?*, 2007, p. 4.

Three elderly men meet at a "Husband's Caring for Their Wives" support group in Wyoming. The Alzheimer's Association estimates men make up nearly 40 percent of all caregivers.

Such false accusations can hurt and frustrate a caregiver, who is working hard to meets the person's needs. Experts urge caregivers not to take paranoia personally but to remember that it is the result of damage from the disease. Psychiatrist and neuropathologist Richard Powers explains: "The content of the delusion has no basis on past life experiences. If the person is arguing about Mom cheating him or Sister stealing from him, people need to understand it isn't necessarily real. It's as if someone took a sledgehammer and smashed your computer and it starts printing out gobbledygook."[26] Instead of arguing about the accusation, offering to look for the item together or distracting the person with another activity brings better results.

Trying to imagine the situation from the patient's point of view can help caregivers understand why a person with AD may react in a way that seems illogical to healthy people. Beth Kallmyer, director of Client and Information Services for the Alzheimer's Association, says, "Imagine that you go to get your wallet right where you left it and it's gone. You positively *know* you didn't move it—because you have no memory of doing that. So the only logical conclusion is that someone else did. That's the reality from the perspective of a person with dementia."[27]

Effects on Caregivers

Besides its devastating effects on people who have the disease, AD takes a heavy toll on caregivers. Caregivers of people with AD and other dementias usually spend more time in their role than caregivers of people with other illnesses, and the care continues for years. Caregivers who have parents with AD often find themselves trying to care for their children and their aging parent at the same time. Spouses and siblings of people with AD may be older and struggling to deal with their own health problems along with caring for their loved one.

In addition to the exhaustion that often goes along with their role, caregivers experience the grief of seeing their loved one's health and mental abilities decline. "It's saddening and disheartening to watch someone you love disappear like that,"[28] comments Greg Kalkwarf, whose grandfather died of AD and whose mother has the disease. Caregivers often suffer from stress, anxiety, and depression. These factors sometimes lead to physical health problems for them.

On the other hand, caregivers also report positive effects from the experience. Taking care of a loved one can bring happiness and a feeling of purpose. One woman who cared for her mother who had AD writes, "I consider that time with her a blessing because I was able to do for her as she did for me,

Caregivers of Alzheimer's patients suffer physical and emotional hardships in caring for relatives. Caregiving also may take a repetitive financial toll.

although it wore out both my husband and me to the point of pure physical exhaustion. I would not trade that time of caring for her for anything."[29]

Help for Caregivers

Caregivers who receive help usually cope better. In some cases, they may be able to arrange for a home health aide to

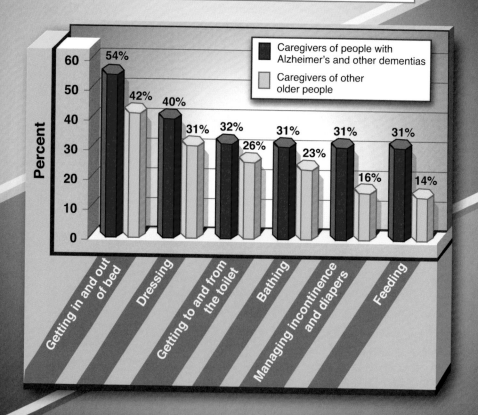

Help With Daily Activities by Caregivers of People with Alzheimer's or Other Dementia vs. Caregivers of Other Older People in the United States (2009)

Legend:
- Caregivers of people with Alzheimer's and other dementias
- Caregivers of other older people

Activity	Caregivers of people with Alzheimer's and other dementias	Caregivers of other older people
Getting in and out of bed	54%	42%
Dressing	40%	31%
Getting to and from the toilet	32%	26%
Bathing	31%	23%
Managing incontinence and diapers	31%	16%
Feeding	31%	14%

Taken from: Data from the 2009 National Alliance for Caregiving/AARP survey on caregiving in the United States, prepared under contract for the Alzheimer's Association by Matthew Greenwald and Associates, November 11, 2009.

handle daily care, such as bathing and dressing the person with AD, and to help with household chores. A visiting nurse may be available to check on the patient and give medications.

Enrolling the person with AD in an adult day-care program can give the caregiver time to handle other necessary matters. These programs give people with AD the chance to socialize with others and take part in enjoyable activities, such as crafts or singing. Some offer exercise as part of the program. Since changes in routine can confuse a person with AD, he or she may need time to adjust to a day-care program.

Studies show that regular exercise relieves stress, improves sleep, and reduces depression in caregivers. Other studies are examining further ways to help caregivers. For example, Resources for Enhancing Alzheimer's Caregiver Health (REACH), a six-month-long study, taught caregivers several strategies, including role playing, problem-solving, stress management techniques, and telephone support groups. At the end of the study, caregivers reported that these strategies made their lives easier and helped them provide better care for their loved ones.

Researchers continue to look for ways to help caregivers and people with AD cope with their challenges and improve their quality of life. Meanwhile, other researchers are trying to uncover the causes of AD in the hope of finding ways to treat or prevent the disease.

CHAPTER FOUR

Changes in the Brain

As the human brain ages, some changes naturally occur. The changes that AD causes are different from those that arise from normal aging. As damage from AD spreads through different parts of the brain, the person loses the abilities that those brain areas handle. Although researchers have discovered much about the way that AD damages the brain, they still do not know why these changes begin.

Activity in a Healthy Brain

A normal, healthy human brain contains 100 billion nerve cells, or neurons. That number is difficult to picture, so this illustration may help: If someone were to count one neuron every second, it would take 3,171 years to count all of the neurons in one human brain. Neurons send messages to each other across the gaps, or synapses, between them. The network of neurons in a human brain contains 100 trillion synapses. Counting one synapse every second would take 3,171,000 years!

Each neuron has a cell body with a long, narrow "arm" called an axon for sending messages to other neurons. Each neuron also has thin dendrites branching out from it to receive messages from other neurons. To send a message, a neuron transmits an electrical signal down its axon. The axon then releases chemicals called neurotransmitters, which carry the message across the synapse. When these chemical messengers reach the next neuron, they fit into receptors on that neuron, the way a key fits into a lock. Most receptors are on the dendrites, but

How Neurons Communicate

- An electrical impulse runs down the **axon**.
- This causes the axon to release chemical messengers, or **neurotransmitters**.
- The neurotransmitters travel across the **synapse**. Each neuron has about a thousand synapses between its axon and the dendrites of other neurons.
- The neurotransmitters reach a **dendrite** of the next neuron.
- The neurotransmitters fit into **receptors** on the dendrite in order to deliver their message.

Illustration of synaptic transmission of a synapse from neuron A (purple) to a dendritic spine of Neuron B (green). The orange spheres are neurotransmitters, which attach themselves to the receptors (red) and open the sodium channels.

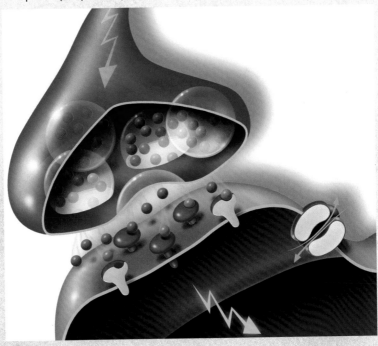

some are also on the cell body. The signal that the neurotransmitters deliver passes through the receiving neuron, which then sends the message down its axon and on to other neurons. All of this happens in the blink of an eye.

Neurons need oxygen, nutrients, and other chemicals to make energy, build proteins, and repair themselves. Blood delivers these materials to the brain as it travels through a network of large blood vessels called arteries that branch off into smaller arteries called arterioles, which branch off again into tiny vessels called capillaries. The brain's transportation network has 400 billion capillaries. The blood also carries away waste products. Between 20 and 25 percent of all the blood that a human heart pumps is directed to the brain.

Natural Changes Versus AD

As the brain ages, some changes are common and expected. The brain's levels of neurotransmitters drop, and some connections between neurons fail to work properly. This makes communication between neurons more difficult. Small blood vessels may become clogged, and fewer new blood vessels form. This results in reduced blood flow to the brain.

These changes can cause memory decline. Usually, the person can still remember information, although it may take a little more time to recall it. The brain is able to compensate for the problem, since different brain areas communicate with each other. If one area is having trouble, other brain areas may handle the tasks.

In a brain stricken with AD, however, the changes are far worse. Neurons die, brain areas shrink, and the damage gradually spreads throughout the brain. When doctors examine brain tissue from patients who have died from AD, they find two types of lesions, or abnormal tissue changes. These lesions, known as amyloid plaques and neurofibrillary tangles, are the same two features that Alois Alzheimer found when he first described the disease in 1906.

Researchers have learned much about plaques and tangles in the hundred years since their discovery, but much remains

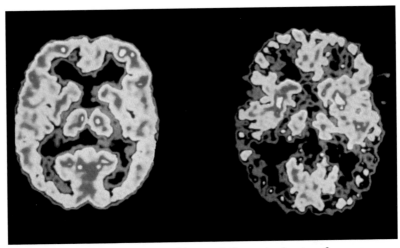

This PET scan shows a normal brain, left, and a brain of an Alzheimer's patient, right. High brain activity is shown in red and yellow and low activity in blue and black. The scan on the right shows reduction of blood flow in Alzheimer's.

a mystery. They still do not know when the damage begins and what triggers it. They believe that it starts long before memory loss and other symptoms arise.

Amyloid Plaques

Amyloid plaques consist of pieces of a protein produced by neurons. Like all cells in the body, neurons make many different kinds of proteins. They do this by stringing together chemicals called amino acids. Twenty different kinds of amino acids play a role in the body. Amino acids can string together in many different sequences to form many different proteins, the way that the letters in the alphabet can string together to form many different words. Each type of protein has its own unique sequence of amino acids. Often, this sequence is hundreds of amino acids long.

The protein involved with the formation of plaques is the amyloid precursor protein (APP). In the middle of the chain of amino acids that make up APP is a section about forty-two amino acids long. This smaller section, called a peptide, is beta-amyloid. If the beta-amyloid peptide gets free from the

Computer artwork showing amyloid proteins on brain tissue (grey).

rest of the APP protein, it can stick to other beta-amyloid peptides and eventually form plaques.

Most of the time, this does not happen. Other proteins known as enzymes cleave, or snip, APP into smaller pieces. When an enzyme known as alpha-secretase cleaves APP, it does so in the middle of the beta-amyloid peptide. This means that beta-amyloid cannot be released into the brain.

The problem occurs when a different enzyme, beta-secretase, cleaves APP. It does so at one end of the beta-amyloid peptide.

Another enzyme, gamma-secretase, then cleaves APP at the other end of the beta-amyloid peptide. As a result, beta-amyloid is released into the brain.

This sticky beta-amyloid peptide attaches to other beta-amyloid peptides that have been released. Up to a dozen of them stick together to form an oligomer. Researchers believe that the brain clears away some oligomers before they can do any damage, but others remain. These clump together with more oligomers and other materials, until they form a plaque in a space between neurons.

Unanswered Questions

Researchers once believed that the plaques caused the damage to the neurons. Now many think that the smaller oligomers may cause the damage by interfering with the signals between neurons. The brain may clump the oligomers together into plaques in an effort to get rid of them. The University of Pittsburgh's William Klunk likens plaques to toxic waste dumps.

Even healthy brains produce some amount of beta-amyloid. Why it forms oligomers and plaques in some brains and not in others is not completely understood. Klunk explains:

> There are two ways that amyloid can go. It can go down the alpha-secretase pathway, and that way you clip the beta-amyloid, 42-amino acid chunk in half, so you can never make beta-amyloid. Or you can go down the non-alpha-secretase pathway, and get the beta and the gamma cleavages, and make beta-amyloid. While we all do both of those, some people think that maybe Alzheimer's patients shunt more of it down the beta-amyloid pathway. But that's not completely clear. What is clear for sure is that all of us do it at least some. And most of us, particularly in our earlier years, clear out what we make. It doesn't build up.[30]

Neurologist Oscar Lopez sums up the current state of knowledge about plaques:

> Nobody knows exactly what is the cause of Alzheimer's disease. However, it seems that the abnormal deposition

of amyloid is the central pathology of the disease. The amyloid is a . . . protein that undergoes an abnormal cleavage. These abnormal proteins are released to the body, and consequently, they start accumulating in the brain. But how this is happening, why this is happening, nobody knows.[31]

A Combination of Factors

One factor that makes the situation even more confusing is that some people who accumulate beta-amyloid in their brains do not develop AD symptoms. Researchers who are conducting studies with new brain imaging techniques are finding plaques in healthy, living people. Pathologists who conduct autopsies also find plaques in patients who have died from other causes. Klunk reports that "above age 65, probably a quarter of the people have detectable amyloid. And it's usually small levels, not to be confused with the levels we see in Alzheimer's disease. But as you get into very elderly persons, like above age 85, close to half of the people have levels of amyloid that are detectable through the kind of brain imaging that we do."[32]

In most of these cases, the plaques are fewer in healthy people than in people with AD. Klunk adds:

> If you gave me ten brain scans of elderly people who have some amyloid and ten Alzheimer's patients, I could probably separate all ten of those. Maybe I would miss one either way. But there are a few, like that one in ten, that might look just like an Alzheimer's patient. They have just as much amyloid as an Alzheimer's patient, but they have no symptoms. So it's a clear message that the amyloid isn't the only thing. It's not a situation where if you have one unit of amyloid in your brain, you have one unit of memory loss. There are mediators.[33]

Possible mediators, or factors that trigger an effect, are vascular problems, such as heart disease, stroke, or diabetes. People who have these conditions along with plaques are

Types of Memory

Different brain areas handle different types of memory, and AD does not damage all of these at the same time. Short-term memory allows a person to recall information for a few seconds up to a few hours. It includes the ability to recall recent events, such as where a person parked the car or whether one turned on the stove. In AD, the damage begins in brain areas involved with short-term memory.

Other types of memory are affected later, when the damage has spread to other parts of the brain. Semantic memory involves knowledge of facts, concepts, and words. For example, semantic memory allows a person to recite the alphabet or remember who George Washington was. Implicit, or procedural, memory allows a person to recall information stored in the subconscious in order to perform familiar tasks automatically. Implicit memory allows a person to do such things as ride a bike, drive a car, get dressed, or make a sandwich without having to consciously think about how to do it every time.

more likely to develop AD symptoms. Klunk continues, "So it seems that it's this mixture of at least plaques plus something else. Vascular problems are an important one; there are probably others that we don't understand quite as well that go into the final display of symptoms."[34] He also reports that people who have high levels of beta-amyloid but who show no AD symptoms usually have few or none of the second hallmark of AD—neurofibrillary tangles.

Neurofibrillary Tangles

Unlike amyloid plaques, which form between neurons, neurofibrillary tangles form inside neurons. Each neuron has microscopic tubes that extend down its axon. The neuron transports its nutrients, neurotransmitters, and other materials through these tubes. A chemical called a tau protein binds to the tubes to keep their structure strong and stable.

Normally, these threads of tau protein have phosphorus molecules attached to them. In a brain afflicted with AD, a greater amount of phosphorus attaches to the tau. This causes the tau threads to unstick from the tubes they were helping to support. A loose tau thread becomes entangled with other loose tau threads, to form the neurofibrillary tangles that Alois Alzheimer described. As a result, the tubes collapse. With its transport system disrupted, the neuron can no longer move materials or communicate with other neurons. These damaged neurons soon die.

A colored electron micrograph of an Alzheimer's damaged brain cell. The neurofibrillary tangle is shown in dark blue lying in the green cytoplasm of the cell body.

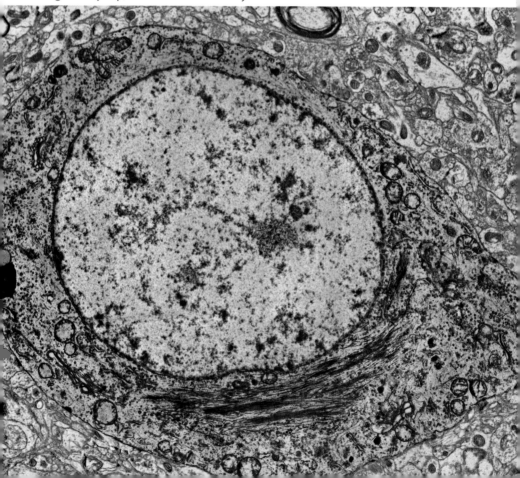

Devastating Results

Although beta-amyloid and neurofibrillary tangles damage neurons, researchers still are unsure whether they are a cause or a result of AD. Lopez says, "It is possible that the tangles and amyloid deposition are the end of a pathological cascade. We know that the amyloid oligomers are toxic to the brain, and it could be that these circulating oligomers are the cause of neuronal toxicity, not the plaque. If you put neurons and oligomers in a petri dish, the oligomers are toxic to the neurons."[35]

Whatever the cause of AD, the results are clear. Communication between neurons is lost, and damaged neurons die. As more neurons die in a certain brain area, that area atrophies, or shrinks. The fluid-filled spaces, or ventricles, between brain areas enlarge. The person gradually loses memory and other thinking abilities, and the symptoms get worse as physical damage spreads to other areas. Since different brain areas handle different tasks, not all abilities are affected at the same time.

The Damage Spreads

Researchers believe that the damage AD causes to the brain may begin ten to twenty years before outward symptoms appear. It starts in the entorhinal cortex, a brain area important to memory. From there, it spreads to the hippocampus, a brain area involved with learning and converting short-term memories to long-term memories.

As more neurons die and the damage spreads to other brain areas, memory problems and other symptoms appear. In this mild AD stage, the changes in the brain cause people to become confused and to take longer to complete tasks. They begin to lose skills that require planning and organizing, such as paying bills and managing medications. Because brain areas that handle short-term memory are affected, sufferers may not remember new information but still recall details from many years before.

The damage then spreads to brain areas involved with other functions. These areas control reasoning and conscious thought, allow people to use and understand language, and

Plaques and tangles eventually spread throughout the brain, and patients do not recognize anyone. They depend on others to feed, dress, and bathe them.

handle sensory processing, which is the way the brain receives and understands information that the senses gather. Sensory processing enables people to interpret what is going on both inside their bodies and in the environment around them.

Damage to these brain areas results in the symptoms of moderate AD, which causes people to have trouble using language, reading, and writing. They may lose their impulse control and do inappropriate things that they would never have done before, such as swearing or undressing in public. Other behavioral problems, such as agitation, wandering, hallucination, and delusions, may appear. Meanwhile, the symptoms that began in the mild stage continue to worsen.

Plaques and tangles eventually spread throughout the brain. In this severe AD stage, patients do not recognize anyone and cannot handle even the most basic tasks. They depend on others to feed, dress, and bathe them. Patients lose the ability to communicate and may make grunting and moaning noises. They also lose control of their bowels and bladder and may have trouble swallowing.

AD ends with the patient's death. The severe damage from the disease can trigger other problems that contribute to death. For instance, trouble with swallowing can allow food and liquids to enter the lungs. This leads to a type of pneumonia that often proves fatal for AD patients.

Other Possible Factors

While scientists try to learn more about how plaques and tangles damage the brain, they also investigate other factors that could worsen the damage. Some believe that inflammation—an immune system reaction to infection or injury—increases the damage once AD has begun. Another idea is that free radicals—oxygen and nitrogen molecules that combine easily with other molecules—damage neurons.

Doctors cannot reverse the damage done by AD, but they have developed medications that help AD sufferers preserve their mental functioning for months or years longer. In addition, researchers are trying to learn what prompts the damage to begin in the first place.

CHAPTER FIVE

Treatment and the Search for Underlying Causes

What scientists have learned about the way that AD damages the brain has led to the development of strategies that address the symptoms and improve quality of life for AD sufferers. Although there is no cure for AD, medications help slow the progression of the disease and, when necessary, manage problem behaviors. Other therapies help relieve stress and allow people with AD to find ways to express themselves.

Besides treating symptoms, researchers are trying to discover the underlying causes of AD. A study of genetics revealed what triggers the damage to begin in some cases of early-onset AD. This field of research has also provided clues as to what may put a person at risk for developing AD later in life.

Disrupted Communication

Medications currently used to treat AD target a problem that occurs at the synapses, or spaces between neurons. Klunk explains, "Synapses are sites where brain cells communicate with each other. That's a critical event in the brain. And they do that communication through chemical messengers."[36] One of these chemical messengers, or neurotransmitters, is acetylcholine. It helps the brain form memories.

In the 1970s, when awareness about AD was rising, researchers discovered that levels of acetylcholine were lower in people with AD. The reason is that an enzyme (a protein that speeds up a chemical reaction) called acetylcholinesterase breaks down acetylcholine. This prevents the neurotransmitter from delivering its message.

In the cholinergic synapse, impulses are transmitted by acetylcholine (Ach, brown and blue ball) that is provided by acetylcoenzyme-S-CoA (yellow). The rate of acetylcholine production is reduced in Alzheimer's patients.

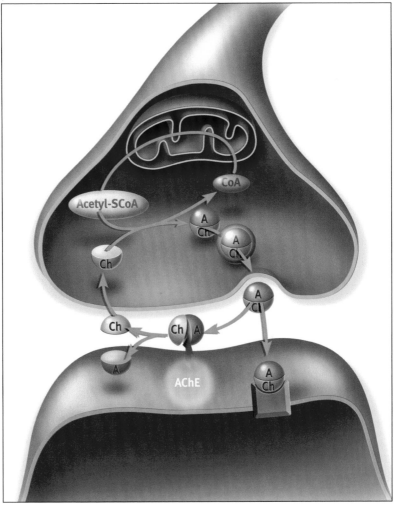

This discovery led scientists to develop drugs that stop or slow down this enzyme in order to prevent it from interfering with communication between neurons. These drugs are called cholinesterase inhibitors. Although their action in the brain is not completely understood, Klunk explains how doctors believe they address the problem:

> Usually one neuron shoots out acetylcholine onto its neighboring neuron, the neighboring neuron gets the message, and the acetylcholinesterase of the synaptic cleft chews up the rest of the message and the message is over. Well, it's sort of crude, but if you inhibit that acetylcholinesterase enzyme, then the message stays there longer. And it has more of an effect. And even though that isn't an exact replacement for the physiology, it still can be beneficial.[37]

Cholinesterase Inhibitors

The first medication that the U.S. Food and Drug Administration (FDA) approved for treating AD symptoms was tacrine (brand name Cognex) in 1993. Doctors prescribed this cholinesterase inhibitor for mild to moderate AD. It is no longer used because its side effects, which include possible liver damage, are more serious than those of later cholinesterase inhibitors. Another disadvantage is that it had to be taken four times a day, compared with once or twice a day for others.

Over the following years, the FDA approved three other cholinesterase inhibitors that doctors currently prescribe for AD. In 1996, donepezil (Aricept) was approved for mild to moderate AD and was later also approved for severe AD. Rivastigmine (Exelon), which was approved in 2000, and galantamine (Razadyne), approved in 2001, treat mild to moderate AD.

Cholinesterase inhibitors do not cure AD or reverse the damage, but they may allow people with AD to preserve their mental functioning longer. Neurologist Oscar Lopez points out, "They are not magic pills. They are not restoring function; they are symptomatic treatments. And they do what they're supposed to do—slow down progression."[38] In AD patients for whom cholinesterase inhibitors prove effective, the drugs keep symptoms from worsening for an average of six to twelve months. A minority of patients appear to benefit longer. All of the cholinesterase inhibitors work in the same way, but an individual patient may respond better to one than to another.

A Drug to Protect Neurons

While cholinesterase inhibitors help increase levels of the chemical messenger acetylcholine, a different type of medication helps regulate levels of another chemical messenger. Glutamate is also a neurotransmitter involved with memory. Neurons damaged by AD release larger than normal amounts of glutamate. When glutamate attaches itself to receptors on a neuron in order to deliver its message, it allows calcium to enter that neuron. The calcium plays a role in helping the neuron store information. If glutamate levels are too high, an unhealthy amount of calcium enters the neuron and contributes to damage.

Since 1993 the FDA has approved only four cholinesterase inhibitor drugs that inhibit the breakdown of acetylcholine.

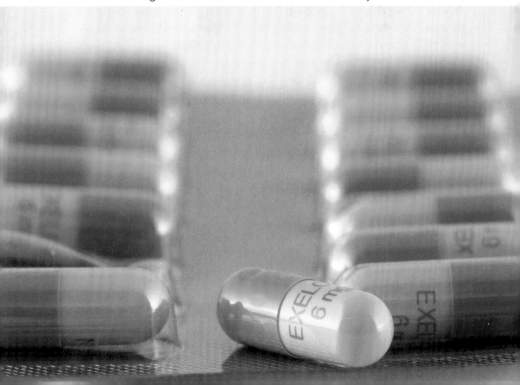

In 2003, the FDA approved memantine (Namenda), a drug developed to address this problem. Doctors believe that memantine protects neurons by blocking glutamate from entering these receptors. They prescribe it to patients with moderate to severe AD. As is true with the cholinesterase inhibitors, memantine does not cure AD or reverse the damage, but it can help slow progression of the disease. A patient can take both memantine and a cholinesterase inhibitor at the same time.

Managing Behavior and Psychiatric Symptoms

Cholinesterase inhibitors and memantine are the only drugs specifically approved for treating AD. Other drugs are available for treating problems with mood and behavior that often arise in AD patients. Between 70 and 90 percent of AD patients experience behavioral symptoms. When the symptoms become severe, or when they create a dangerous situation, doctors prescribe medications.

Depression is common in people with AD. Doctors may prescribe one of several different antidepressant medications to address the problem. Some of the most common ones are classified as selective serotonin reuptake inhibitors (SSRIs), because they help regulate levels of the neurotransmitter serotonin.

Problems such as agitation, aggression, hallucination, and delusions can cause much distress for people with AD and for their caregivers. Doctors often prescribe antipsychotic medications to control hallucinations and delusions in people with other disorders, and these medications may also help control agitation and other mood problems. In people with dementia, however, antipsychotics have been found to carry an increased risk of stroke and death.

Experts recommend other methods of handling these behavior problems in dementia patients, such as identifying and addressing the underlying cause and finding ways to distract or reassure the person. If these methods fail, and if the behavior

FDA-Approved Drugs for Treating Alzheimer's Disease

Generic Name	Brand Name	Type of Drug	Year Approved	Stage of AD	Common Side Effects
tacrine*	Cognex*	cholinesterase inhibitor	1993	mild to moderate	nausea, diarrhea, vomiting, possible liver damage
donepezil	Aricept	cholinesterase inhibitor	1996	originally approved for mild to moderate; later also aproved for severe	nausea, diarrhea, vomiting, loss of appetite
rivastigmine	Exelon	cholinesterase inhibitor	2000	mild to moderate	nausea, diarrhea, vomiting, loss of appetite, muscle weakness
galantamine	Razadyne	cholinesterase inhibitor	2001	mild to moderate	nausea, vomiting, diarrhea, loss of appetite
memantine	Namenda	glutamate blocker	2003	moderate to severe	headache, constipation, confusion, dizziness

* Most doctors no longer prescribe this drug for AD due to potentially dangerous side effects.

is severe or dangerous, doctors may prescribe a low dose of an antipsychotic medication. Some doctors prescribe a low dose of another type of medication known as a mood stabilizer instead. Mood stabilizers are mostly used to treat mood swings and agitation in people with bipolar disorder, commonly called manic depression.

Sleep problems are also common. When people with AD cannot sleep through the night, this can create a dangerous situation. For instance, they may wander, turn on the stove, or get into other dangerous situations while caregivers are sleeping. This adds to the stress on caregivers and often prevents them from getting a good night's sleep. Strategies for handling the problem include keeping the same bedtime every night, helping the person stay active earlier in the day, and limiting caffeine. Sleeping aids may increase confusion in people with AD, especially if these interact with other medications the person is taking. Some sleeping aids lead to physical dependence. For these reasons, doctors usually prescribe sleeping aids to AD patients only after nondrug strategies have failed.

The Importance of Exercise

Another strategy for managing symptoms is regular exercise. Studies show that exercise helps preserve cognitive abilities, and it also improves mood and helps fight depression. Exercise earlier in the day can help combat sleep problems, because the person will feel tired at night. It also improves overall physical health.

People with AD may find exercise a challenge, but exercise does not have to be strenuous to yield good results. It can take the form of a short walk with a caregiver. When people with AD and their caregivers exercise together, both experience healthful results. Lopez says, "In addition to the medications [such as cholinesterase inhibitors and memantine],

Regular exercise helps manage symptoms. When a caregiver and patient exercise together, both can experience positive results.

exercise and cognitive activity can help to improve cognition. Even walking four blocks per day is critical." He summarizes recommended treatments by adding, "The best thing is to make sure that the person has a healthy lifestyle, stays active, and takes the medications that we have now for Alzheimer's disease."[39]

Helpful Activities

Other nonmedical therapies can enrich the lives of people with AD. Because of the damage AD causes to the brain, people with this disease often have trouble communicating, and they may no longer be able to participate in activities they once enjoyed. AD patients benefit from activities that bring meaning to their lives and that allow them to interact with others.

Art is often used as a therapy. Painting, drawing, or simple craft projects can give people with AD a sense of accomplishment and a way to express themselves. Music therapy helps people to relax and improves sleep and other behavioral problems. It includes music familiar to the person, perhaps from the past. People with AD are encouraged to participate by singing and moving to the music.

Because people with AD may still remember details from the past when the present has become confusing, reminiscence therapy can be comforting. It involves activities such as looking at old photographs, watching old movies or television shows the person once enjoyed, and asking the person to tell about events from the past.

Reading to the person can also provide enjoyment. Some short books have been written especially for people who have dementia. Peter V. Rabins, codirector of the Division of Geriatric Psychiatry and Neuropsychiatry at the Johns Hopkins University School of Medicine, notes, "Anything that helps make it easier for people to interact produces benefits in both directions—the family member with the disease and the caregiver. It gives the person with the disease a chance to interact with grandkids or younger children. It's positive both ways."[40]

Genetic Clues

In addition to treating symptoms, researchers are trying to discover the underlying causes of AD. They hope that this will allow them to develop ways to prevent AD and to identify people who are at risk. They know that amyloid plaques and neurofibrillary tangles form in the brains of people with AD and that the disease damages and kills neurons. At present, they do not know why this damage begins. One factor that researchers are investigating is the role that genetics plays.

In some cases of early-onset AD, researchers have uncovered evidence that the disease is inherited. Klunk notes, "The only situation where we have a really good idea of what causes Alzheimer's disease is in those rare families—and I'm talking about less than one percent of all people with Alzheimer's disease—that carry one of a specific group of mutations."[41]

Those mutations appear in certain chromosomes—long strings of genes that are coiled up into packages inside cells. Normally, people inherit twenty-three chromosomes from their mother and twenty-three from their father, for a total of forty-six, or twenty-three pairs of chromosomes. One pair of these chromosomes determines whether the person is male or female. The other pairs are identified by numbers, from one to twenty-two.

Each chromosome contains thousands of genes. These genes give cells instructions on how to make proteins. If a mutation, or permanent change in a gene, occurs, the instructions are delivered incorrectly, and the cells may make an abnormal form of the protein.

Dangerous Mutations

To determine the role that genes play in AD, researchers studied families in which an unusually large number of people developed early-onset AD. They discovered mutations on three different chromosomes. In some families, sufferers inherited gene mutations on chromosome 21. In others, a mutation occurred on chromosome 14 or chromosome 1.

All of these mutations affect production of beta-amyloid, the protein pieces that clump together to form plaques between neurons. The mutations on chromosome 21 instruct cells to make an abnormal form of the larger protein that beta-amyloid comes from. The mutations on chromosomes 14 and

Genetic Testing

People born to families in which early-onset AD is passed on through a genetic mutation have a 50/50 chance of inheriting the disease. They face a difficult question: Should they take a genetic test that will reveal whether or not they have inherited the mutation?

Even though a negative test result would bring great relief, many issues arise when a test comes back positive. Experts recommend that anyone considering the test first go through genetic counseling, since learning the results may have a huge impact not only on the person being tested but also on the spouse, children, and other family members.

Many people choose not to be tested, feeling that since the disease cannot be cured at present, there would be no benefit in receiving the devastating news of a positive result. Others want to know because it may affect their decisions about having children or so they can participate in research studies to fight the disease.

A man who tested positive for an AD mutation at age thirty-one said, "Not knowing if you have the mutation is just as bad as knowing that you have it. Either you spend your life in denial or you spend it in angst and panic wondering if you'll get it. We know the risk is 50 percent. That's huge! If you find out you will get it—well, you probably expected as much anyway, so now you can start dealing with it."[1]

1 affect an enzyme that snips this larger protein into smaller pieces to release beta-amyloid. Klunk sums up the results: "These folks produce a lot of a slightly more sticky form of the amyloid beta protein, and they get build-up of plaques in their brains in their 30s and 40s, and they get Alzheimer's in their 40s and 50s. So in that case we know it's the gene mutations that are causing the amyloid disregulation and it's leading to Alzheimer's."[42]

On the other hand, a twenty-six-year-old woman decided against being tested. She said, "If I knew I carried the mutation, I would not be able to get up in the morning."[2]

1. Quoted in Gabrielle Strobel. "Interview: One Man's Forward Approach," Alzheimer Research Forum, June 11, 2007. www.alzforum.org/eFAD/profiles/approach.asp.
2. Quoted in Gabrielle Strobel. "Genetic Testing and Counseling for Early-Onset Familial Alzheimer Disease," Alzheimer Research Forum, May 17, 2007. www .alzforum.org/eFAD/diagenetics/essay4/essay4.asp.

Doctors scan a DNA pattern on an X-ray for genetic markers that could be associated with a defective gene that may be the cause of familial Alzheimer's disease.

This also explains a link between AD and Down syndrome, a condition that slows mental and physical development in children. Most people with Down syndrome develop AD symptoms by age 40. Although people normally have two copies of each chromosome, people with Down syndrome have three copies of chromosome 21. This is the same chromosome that carries the genetic mutations that trigger early-onset AD in some families.

Inheritance Pattern

With some hereditary diseases, inheriting a certain gene or gene mutation does not necessarily mean that the person will develop the disease. It may simply mean that the person's chances of developing the disease are greater if the right combination of circumstances should arise. With other hereditary diseases, a person must inherit the mutation from both parents in order to develop the disease.

With the mutations on chromosomes 1, 14, and 21 that cause early-onset AD, the situation is more serious. This form of the disease is autosomal dominant, meaning that AD will develop even if the person inherits the mutation from only one parent.

Because chromosomes come in pairs, one from each parent, a person who inherited the disease from a parent has one normal copy of the gene and one mutation. For example, he may have one normal chromosome 14 and one chromosome 14 that carries the gene mutation. A child born to that person then has a 50 percent chance of inheriting the normal chromosome and a 50 percent chance of inheriting the mutation that will lead to early-onset AD. "It's early-onset with a specific inheritance pattern, so that 50 percent of every generation will get this gene," Klunk says. "Because it's autosomal dominant, you have a 50/50 chance of getting the bad gene from the parent, and it only takes one diseased gene to cause the disease."[43]

The discovery that genetic mutations cause early-onset AD in certain families was a breakthrough, but it did not explain other cases of early-onset AD. Klunk adds, "Of those people who are really early, less than age 50, we can identify one of these gene mutations in only about half of those people. Half don't have a gene mutation at all or if they have a mutation we haven't been able to identify it yet."[44]

Genes and Late-Onset AD

These mutations also do not explain late-onset AD, the far more common form of the disease. People who develop late-onset AD do not have the gene mutations on chromosomes 1, 14, or 21. Researchers have not found a gene that by itself causes late-onset AD, but they have found certain genes that appear to increase a person's risk for developing the disease.

This is a fragment of an apolipoprotein E molecule. The only gene found to have a significant effect on a person's chance of developing late-onset AD contains the instructions for building this molecule.

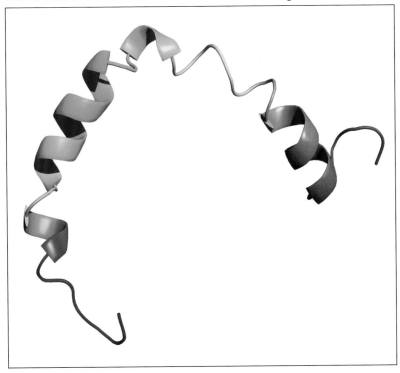

So far, the only gene found to have a significant effect on a person's chances of developing late-onset AD is a gene on chromosome 19. Because this gene contains instructions for making a protein called apolipoprotein E (APOE), it is known as the APOE gene. This gene comes in several forms, including those written as APOE ε2, APOE ε3, and APOE ε4.

APOE ε3 is the most common form, and it appears to have no effect on whether or not a person develops AD. APOE ε2 is rarer, and studies lead researchers to believe that it may provide some protection against AD. These studies showed that when people who have APOE ε2 get AD, they usually get it at a later age than people who have APOE ε4.

About 25 to 30 percent of people in general have APOE ε4, compared with 40 percent of late-onset AD patients. Because a higher percentage of people with AD have APOE ε4, researchers believe that this form of the gene increases a person's risk for developing the disease. Having APOE ε4 does not in itself mean that a person will develop AD. Rather, its presence may make it more likely that the disease will develop if the right combination of other factors occurs. Many people who have this form of the gene never develop AD, and a large number of people with AD do not have APOE ε4.

Because people who have a close relative with AD develop the disease more often than people who do not, researchers believe that other AD risk-factor genes exist. These genes have much less of an effect than APOE ε4, which makes them difficult to identify. In order to find them, researchers must study the genes of thousands of people who have a close relative with AD and compare these with the genes of thousands of other people. By 2010, researchers had identified several other risk-factor genes suspected to have only a minimal effect. If a person were to inherit several of these genes, their combined effect could be more significant.

Risk Factors

Aside from those rare cases involving gene mutations, scientists are still struggling to understand what triggers the damage from AD in the first place. With this complex disease, finding the answer is not as simple as identifying a single cause. Risk-factor genes are only one piece of the puzzle.

Experts believe that a combination of factors, including genetics, environment, and lifestyle, could put a person at risk. The way that these factors come into play over a lifetime may make the difference between whether or not a person develops AD. Researchers are searching for ways to lower the risk.

CHAPTER SIX

The Continuing Battle Against a Complex Disease

Because AD may be caused by a complex combination of factors, researchers are studying many different strategies to fight the disease. Some efforts are aimed at prevention. Researchers hope that by learning more about the risk factors for AD, they may be able to reduce the risk or prevent the disease from developing.

Others work to develop new treatments for AD. Current medications simply treat the symptoms. Researchers are testing other strategies designed to target the beta-amyloid and tau proteins involved with AD brain damage.

Other research involves finding ways to diagnose AD sooner. This would allow patients to receive treatment or take preventive measures at an earlier stage. It would also allow scientists to gain insight into how the damage begins and progresses.

Research on Reducing Risk Factors

Learning about the conditions under which people are more likely to develop AD can provide clues as to what causes the disease and how it may be prevented. An epidemiologic study observes what people do during their everyday lives that may be associated with the development and/or spread of a disease. Epidemiologic studies are one tool researchers use to examine possible risk factors or preventive measures for AD. They try to determine whether there is a link between AD and the factor being studied.

Vascular disease, including heart disease, stroke, and diabetes, can decrease blood flow to the brain. Epidemiologic studies have examined whether or not vascular disease increases a person's risk for AD. When these studies compared people with and without vascular disease, they found that a higher percentage of people with vascular disease develop AD and other cognitive problems.

This raises the question of whether or not controlling the factors that put a person at risk for vascular disease can also

Researchers are studying vascular diseases to find out whether the diseases increase a person's risk for AD.

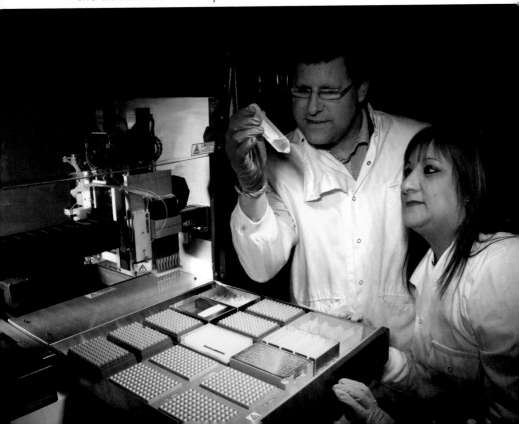

decrease a person's risk for developing AD. The risk factors for vascular disease include high blood pressure, obesity, high levels of triglycerides (fats in the blood), and insulin resistance (a condition that leads to high levels of the hormone insulin in the blood). Ongoing studies are testing whether treatments for these conditions may also lower a person's risk for AD.

Examining the Effects of Exercise

Different types of studies are examining how exercise may affect a person's risk for developing AD. In epidemiologic studies, older people who reported higher levels of physical activity also showed a reduced risk for dementia. For example, in a six-year study involving seventeen hundred people aged sixty-five and older, researchers compared those who exercised at least three times a week with those who exercised less frequently. The ones who exercised more showed a 35 to 40 percent lower risk for AD.

In their everyday lives, people have a variety of different practices and habits. This makes it difficult to determine whether the results of an epidemiologic study are caused by the factor being studied—such as exercise—or by other factors. On the other hand, a clinical trial is a study that takes place in a controlled setting. One purpose is to rule out the possibility that some other factor may be responsible for the results.

Clinical trials are also examining how exercise may affect a person's risk for AD and other types of cognitive decline. For example, one clinical trial put healthy older adults on a program of brisk walking. After six months, brain scans showed increased activity in certain parts of their brains, compared with activity in the brains of those who were physically inactive.

Studying Diet, Supplements, and Medications

Other studies are aimed at the effects of diet. Two epidemiologic studies published in 2009 suggested that people who

Epidemiological studies have suggested that people who follow a Mediterranean diet may have a lower risk of cognitive decline.

follow a Mediterranean diet may have a lower risk for cognitive decline. This type of diet is low in red meats and sweets and high in vegetables, legumes, fruits, grains, and olive oil. It includes moderately high amounts of fish and seafood and low to moderate amounts of poultry, eggs, dairy products, and red wine. Two other epidemiologic studies found an association between eating more vegetables—especially green, leafy vegetables—and lower rates of cognitive decline.

Scientists are also investigating the possible effects of certain foods or supplements. These include antioxidants, such as vitamins A and E. Highly reactive oxygen and nitrogen molecules known as free radicals can damage cells. Some researchers believe that free radicals play a role in the brain damage that AD patients experience. Because antioxidants bind to free radicals and prevent them from damaging cells, researchers want to learn whether antioxidants can lower a person's risk for AD.

Clinical trials have not yet found evidence that antioxidants protect against AD or other forms of memory loss, but the investigation continues. One large clinical trial, the Prevention of Alzheimer's Disease by Vitamin E and Selenium (PREAD-VISE), is following more than ten thousand older men over a period of seven to twelve years.

Another supplement under study is ginkgo biloba. Some people take this herb in the hopes that it will prevent AD. So far, clinical trials have not shown this result. "It just is very solid that it doesn't work as a preventive treatment for Alzheimer's disease,"[45] neurologist Oscar Lopez says.

Besides damage from free radicals, some researchers believe that inflammation may play a role in the damage AD does to the brain. This has led them to investigate the effects that nonsteroidal anti-inflammatory drugs (NSAIDs), such as ibuprofen and naproxen, may have on the prevention of AD. Some studies have suggested that taking NSAIDs may reduce a person's risk for AD, but clinical trials have not found evidence to support this. Scientists are still investigating the possible effects of these drugs on AD.

Brain-Stimulating Activities

In addition to physical factors, scientists are studying whether keeping mentally active may affect a person's risk for AD. Several studies show a relationship between activities that engage the brain and a lower risk for AD. For example, one four-year study compared older people who frequently took part in brain-stimulating activities, such as reading newspapers, doing crossword puzzles, and going to museums, with older people who did such things less frequently. When the investigators compared the number of people in each group that developed AD, they found a 47 percent lower risk in the group that frequently did the brain-stimulating activities.

Some studies suggest that people who have more social ties have a decreased risk for cognitive decline. Others show a link with education. In these studies, people with more years of education appeared to have a decreased risk for dementia.

Researchers are trying to figure out the meaning of these results. One explanation is that such factors as brain-stimulating activity, social engagement, and education may help the brain to become more adaptable. That way, if problems arise with certain brain areas, other areas can find ways to compensate.

Another possibility is that factors such as lower mental and social engagement are not a cause of the disease but, rather, an effect of it. Some study participants who took part in fewer social and mental activities may have done so because AD had already taken hold in their brains. They may have been experiencing the effects of the disease at a stage that was too early to be diagnosed.

In the studies involving education, researchers are also unsure what is responsible for the effect. People who receive more education often also have better financial circumstances and access to better health care. These other factors, rather than the education itself, could be responsible for the results.

A recent study indicated that older people who frequently took part in brain-stimulating activities, such as reading newspapers, doing crossword puzzles, and going to museums, had a 47 percent lower risk of cognitive loss.

Association Versus Cause

Even when evidence shows that a factor is associated with the risk for AD, this does not necessarily mean that it causes AD or that controlling it will prevent the disease. Martha L. Daviglus, professor of medicine and preventive medicine at Northwestern University, explains, "These associations are examples of the classic chicken or the egg quandary. Are people able to stay mentally sharp over time because they are physically active and socially engaged or are they simply more likely to stay physically active and socially engaged because they are mentally sharp? An association only tells us that these things are related, not that one causes the other."[46] More research is needed to shed light on the relationship between AD and possible risk factors.

Although experts cannot say for sure that controlling diet, exercise, or other factors will help prevent AD, some of these strategies carry other benefits. For example, exercise and lowering high blood pressure are good for a person's physical health. Social and brain-stimulating activities can help a person to enjoy life and are good for mental and emotional health.

On the other hand, some strategies that are claimed to prevent AD can lead to harm. The Alzheimer's Disease Education and Referral Center at the National Institute on Aging offers this caution:

> Because AD is such a devastating disease, caregivers and patients may be tempted by untried, unproven, and unscientific cures, supplements, or prevention strategies. Check with your doctor before trying pills or any other prescription or non-prescription treatment that promises to prevent AD. These purchases might be unsafe or a waste of money. They might even interfere with other medical treatments that have been prescribed.[47]

The Search for Risk-Factor Genes

While some researchers look for risk factors that can be controlled, others continue to search for genes that increase a

Evaluating the Results of Prevention Studies

In 2010, researchers at the Duke Evidence-Based Practice Center reviewed the results of Alzheimer's prevention studies. They tried to determine whether these studies had found convincing evidence that certain factors increase or decrease a person's risk for AD.

The review found evidence that diabetes, smoking, depression, and the presence of the APOE ε4 gene are associated with an increased risk for AD and cognitive decline. The researchers also reported that a Mediterranean-style diet, cognitive engagement, and physical activities appear to be associated with a decreased risk for AD and cognitive decline.

The researchers cautioned that the findings of these studies were not always strong. They also pointed out that even though they did not see evidence for an association between the risk for AD and other factors, such as use of nonsteroidal anti-inflammatory drugs (NSAIDs) or antioxidants, that does not mean that these factors can be ruled out. Further research may turn up evidence that these are significant.

person's risk for AD. To find these genes, researchers collect blood samples. They compare samples from AD patients and healthy people, or from people who have close family members with AD and those who do not. One large program, the Alzheimer's Disease Genetics Consortium, began in 2007 to allow many genetics researchers to work together. Their goal is to collect samples from ten thousand people with AD and the same number of healthy people for comparison.

Finding these genes could help doctors identify people who are at risk. It could also help researchers to better understand the causes of AD and to find strategies to prevent or treat the disease. For example, if a gene is found to increase a person's risk for AD, and that gene carries instructions for building a certain protein, that would provide a clue that this protein may be involved with the development of AD. Researchers may then be able to come up with a treatment that addresses the problem. Klunk explains: "The reason we want to learn about genes is that we want to learn more about the biology behind those genes, which can then give us new direct targets to find new drugs that may have an impact on whether the disease develops at all."[48]

Targeting Beta-Amyloid

Some new drugs being tested target beta-amyloid, the protein that builds up to form plaques in the brains of AD patients. Scientists are examining the effects of drugs that they hope will stop beta-amyloid from forming or from clumping together. Other drugs under study are designed to remove beta-amyloid from the brain. Scientists are also examining the question of whether the plaques themselves or earlier forms of beta-amyloid cause the damage.

Researchers often test new AD drugs on transgenic (genetically modified) mice. These mice have genes implanted that trigger their brains to produce large amounts of beta-amyloid. As a result, the mice's brains develop AD-like plaques. One approach first tested on transgenic mice was active immunization against beta-amyloid.

An example of active immunization is the chickenpox vaccine. A doctor injects a child with a weakened form of the chickenpox virus. This triggers the child's immune system to produce antibodies to fight that virus. Similarly, when researchers injected transgenic mice with a vaccine containing beta-amyloid, the mice's immune systems produced antibodies to fight beta-amyloid. As a result of the action of these antibodies, the number of plaques in the mice's brains decreased.

Overcoming an Obstacle

Researchers hoped that the vaccine would have the same effect in humans. A clinical trial began but had to be stopped in

2002 because 15 of the 360 participants developed severe brain inflammation. Their immune systems had responded to the vaccine by producing not only antibodies but also other cells that caused the inflammation.

To get around this problem, researchers developed a different approach. They next tried passive immunization. Instead of triggering the immune system to produce antibodies, passive immunization involves injecting already existing antibodies directly into patients. Klunk elaborates: "Passive immunization would be equivalent to what a breast-feeding infant gets from its mother, when it gets antibodies in the milk. You just get the antibodies; you don't stimulate the immune system."[49]

After smaller studies examined the safety of passive immunization, larger studies began. By 2010, several large clinical trials were under way. Collecting the data and analyzing the results will take a few years.

Targeting Tau

Other drugs are being tested to address the other type of AD lesion, neurofibrillary tangles, which are made of the protein tau. Tangles form after too many phosphorus molecules bind to tau. Some of the new drugs are designed to prevent this from happening. As with drugs for beta-amyloid, drugs that address tau are often tested on transgenic mice. These mice have been genetically altered to form tau tangles either alone or along with beta-amyloid plaques.

Some work with transgenic mice suggests that tau causes damage at an earlier stage, before tangles form. If that is the case, treatments that target tangles may act too late, after the damage is already done. Lopez says, "Many investigators are working on disease modifying treatments that can actually get rid of the brain lesions or arrest the pathological process. But the problem that we're facing is that we don't know what is causing Alzheimer's disease."[50]

Studies on drugs that address tau are in earlier phases than studies on drugs targeting amyloid. Even if these treatments are successful in removing plaques and tangles, that does not

Some researchers working with transgenic mice (shown here), injected with green fluorescing protein, suggest that tau protein causes damage before neurofibrillary tangles form.

necessarily mean that they will cure or prevent AD. Researchers may discover that plaques and tangles are only later results of the disease and that treatment needs to begin earlier in order to be effective.

Looking Inside the Brain

To determine whether new treatments are working and how early they must begin, researchers need to see what happens inside the brains of patients. "The only way to study amyloid in the past was after a person died, and you could open the brain and see the amyloid,"[51] Lopez notes. One drawback of an autopsy is that it shows the damage only at one point in time, but it does not reveal how the damage progressed. New brain imaging techniques are helping researchers solve this problem.

One technique involves a radioactive tracer known as Pittsburgh Compound B. After being injected into a patient, this tracer binds to amyloid in the patient's brain. The brain is then scanned using positron emission tomography, or PET scan, which detects the radioactive tracer and creates a picture on a computer screen. Pittsburgh Compound B shows up in the picture to tell researchers where plaques exist. Klunk, who coinvented the compound, asserts, "It's allowed us for the first time to be able to see the plaque, the pathology, in a living person."[52] Other similar compounds are also being developed.

A PET scan of a brain afflicted with Alzheimer's disease. A radioactive tracer has bonded to amyloid in the patient's brain. Brain activity is confined to the front and back of the brain.

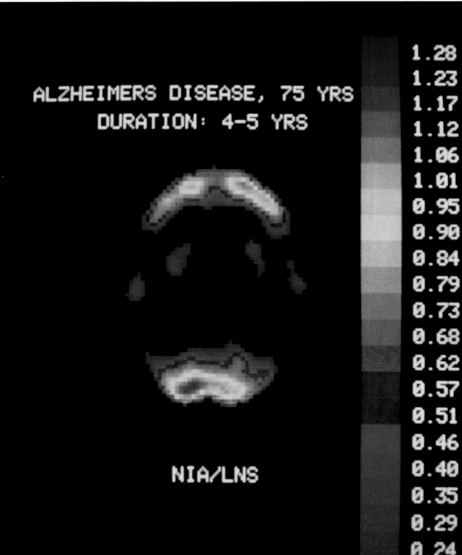

All of these are still in the research stages. If testing is successful, they may become available for doctors to prescribe for diagnosis.

By following patients over time with such tools, researchers will learn how the disease progresses. They will also be able to see how medications affect the course of the disease. They hope that such imaging techniques will not only help develop effective treatments but will also identify people in the very early stages of AD so that doctors can prescribe these treatments in time to prevent the damage. "It's very much a hand-in-glove approach," Klunk explains. "It's hard to develop therapies without being able to see the pathology, but there's not a whole lot of reason to see the pathology that early, until you have drugs that can do something about it. So these are developing hand in hand."[53]

More Research Tools

Measuring amyloid with PET scans is only one method being tested to help scientists learn about AD progression. PET scans can also show the way that the brain uses glucose, a sugar that provides brain cells with energy. A form of glucose with radioactive molecules is injected into a patient, and the PET scan detects it. In AD patients, certain brain areas show decreased glucose metabolism in these scans. Another type of imaging study, magnetic resonance imaging (MRI), uses a magnetic field and sound waves to create a computerized image. Some studies are using MRI to track the way brain areas shrink over time in AD patients.

Cerebrospinal fluid (CSF), a liquid that surrounds the brain and spinal cord, is also providing clues about AD. Doctors use a small needle to withdraw a CSF sample from a patient's lower back. The sample contains brain chemicals, including the beta-amyloid and tau proteins involved with AD. Measuring the amounts of these proteins in CSF may someday allow doctors to diagnose AD at an early stage, perhaps before outward symptoms appear. It could also help track the effects of new medications.

How a New Drug Is Approved

Preclinical studies: An experimental drug is examined in test tubes and animals before being tested on humans.

Clinical trials:
Phase I: A small study, usually involving fewer than a hundred volunteers, that examines the safety of the treatment.

Phase II: A larger study, involving up to several hundred volunteers, that gathers more information about safety, side effects, and dosage. It may offer some indications as to whether the treatment is effective, but the number of participants is too small to provide convincing evidence.

By 2010, treatments aimed at tau proteins were still in Phase I and Phase II.

Phase III: Large studies, involving several hundred or several thousand volunteers, that gather evidence as to whether the treatment is effective and whether the benefits outweigh the risks from side effects. The U.S. Food and Drug Administration (FDA) will examine this evidence when deciding whether or not to approve the drug.

By 2010, some amyloid treatments were already in Phase III. After a drug is approved by the FDA, Phase IV trials gather information about long-term effects.

The Fight Continues

Researchers are studying many other strategies to address AD. In 2010, the Alzheimer's Association reported that more than a hundred research studies targeting AD and related conditions were in progress and recruiting study subjects. Most of these clinical trials were investigating strategies for earlier diagnosis, prevention, and treatment of AD. Some examined ways to help caregivers.

Over a century after Alois Alzheimer first described the disease that came to be named after him, scientists have made great progress in understanding AD. With this complex disease, many questions remain. "We are not slogging through a fog anymore," says Steven Younkin, a neuroscientist at the Mayo Clinic. "We can see the top of the hill for the first time, and while we probably won't get where we want to be for many years, it is really exciting."[54]

Notes

Introduction: Replacing Myths with Knowledge

1. John Pohlod. Interview with the author. September 27, 2010.
2. Pohlod. Interview.
3. Pohlod. Interview.

Chapter One: Exposing an Enemy of Memory

4. Quoted in Barry Petersen. "Jan's Story: Love and Early-Onset Alzheimer's." CBS News, June 20, 2010. www.cbs news.com/stories/2010/06/20/sunday/main6600364.shtml.
5. Quoted in N.C. Berchtold and C.W. Cotman. "Evolution in the Conceptualization of Dementia and Alzheimer's Disease: Greco-Roman Period to the 1960s." *Neurobiology of Aging,* vol. 19, no. 3, 1998, p. 174.
6. Quoted in Berchtold and Cotman. "Evolution in the Conceptualization of Dementia and Alzheimer's Disease: Greco-Roman Period to the 1960s," p. 174.
7. Quoted in Berchtold and Cotman. "Evolution in the Conceptualization of Dementia and Alzheimer's Disease: Greco-Roman Period to the 1960s," pp. 174–175.
8. Quoted in Nawab Qizilbash et al., eds. *Evidence-Based Dementia Practice.* Oxford: Blackwell Science, 2002, p. 209.
9. Quoted in "History of Alzheimer's Disease." Kalamazoo Center for Medical Studies, 2005–2006. http://hod.kcms .msu.edu/timeline.php?y=1901-1906.
10. Quoted in Berchtold and Cotman. "Evolution in the Conceptualization of Dementia and Alzheimer's Disease: Greco-Roman Period to the 1960s," p. 180.

11. Robert Katzman. "The Prevalence and Malignancy of Alzheimer's Disease: A Major Killer." *Archives of Neurology*, April 1976, p. 217.
12. Quoted in "History of Alzheimer's Disease."
13. François Boller and Margaret M. Forbes. "History of Dementia and Dementia in History: An Overview." *Journal of the Neurological Sciences*, vol. 158, 1998, p. 131.

Chapter Two: Diagnosing Alzheimer's Disease

14. Oscar Lopez. Interview with the author, May 20, 2010.
15. William Klunk. Interview with the author, May 17, 2010.
16. Klunk. Interview.
17. Lopez. Interview.
18. Klunk. Interview.
19. Quoted in Randy Dotinga. "Simple Memory Test May Detect Early Alzheimer's." *HealthDay News*, April 8, 2010. www.medicinenet.com/script/main/art.asp?articlekey=115178.
20. Angela Lunde. "Early Diagnosis of Alzheimer's Empowers People." Mayo Clinic, March 4, 2010. www.mayoclinic.com/health/early-diagnosis-of-alzheimers/MY01219.

Chapter Three: Living with Alzheimer's Disease

21. Quoted in R. Morgan Griffin. "What It's Like to Have Dementia." WebMD, 2009. www.webmd.com/brain/features/understanding-dementia-symptoms?page=3.
22. Kathy Hatfield. "What a Spread!" KnowItAlz, March 25, 2010. www.knowitalz.com/community/alzheimer-s/what-a-spread.html.
23. *Caring for a Person with Alzheimer's Disease*. National Institute on Aging, National Institutes of Health, March 2010, p. 12.
24. Stephen Soreff. "Understanding and Dealing with Resident Aggression: Exploring the Extent, Causes, and Impact of Aggressive Outbursts and How to Handle Them." *Nursing Homes*, March 2004. http://findarticles.com/p/articles/mi_m3830/is_3_53/ai_n6066074/.

25. Quoted in Deborah Franklin. "Camp for Alzheimer's Patients Isn't About Memories." National Public Radio, September 6, 2010. www.npr.org/templates/story/story.php?storyId=129607201&ft=1&f=3.

26. Quoted in Dennis Thompson Jr. "Dealing with Hallucinations and Delusions in Alzheimer's." EverydayHealth, December 29, 2008. www.everydayhealth.com/alzheimers/alzheimers-hallucinations-and-delusions.aspx.

27. Quoted in Griffin. "What It's Like to Have Dementia," p. 3.

28. Quoted in Elizabeth Landau. "Children of Alzheimer's Sufferers Want to Know Their Risk." CNN, July 20, 2010. www.cnn.com/2010/HEALTH/07/16/alzheimer.guidelines/index.html.

29. "Barbara's Story." Alzheimer's Association, September 8, 2008. www.alz.org/living_with_alzheimers_14446.asp.

Chapter Four: Changes in the Brain

30. Klunk. Interview.
31. Lopez. Interview.
32. Klunk. Interview.
33. Klunk. Interview.
34. Klunk. Interview.
35. Lopez. Interview.

Chapter Five: Treatment and the Search for Underlying Causes

36. Klunk. Interview.
37. Klunk. Interview.
38. Lopez. Interview.
39. Lopez. Interview.
40. Quoted in "Many Alzheimer's Patients Find Comfort in Books." *New York Times*, April 22, 2010. http://newoldage.blogs.nytimes.com/2010/04/22/many-alzheimers-patients-find-comfort-in-books/.
41. Klunk. Interview.
42. Klunk. Interview.
43. Klunk. Interview.
44. Klunk. Interview.

Chapter Six: The Continuing Battle Against a Complex Disease

45. Lopez. Interview.
46. Quoted in "Independent Panel Finds Insufficient Evidence to Support Preventive Measures for Alzheimer's Disease." *NIH News*, April 28, 2010. www.nih.gov/news/health/apr2010/od-28.htm.
47. National Institutes of Health. *Genes, Lifestyles, and Crossword Puzzles: Can Alzheimer's Disease Be Prevented?*, April 2009, p. 30.
48. Klunk. Interview.
49. Klunk. Interview.
50. Lopez. Interview.
51. Lopez. Interview.
52. Klunk. Interview.
53. Klunk. Interview.
54. Quoted in *Medical News*. "The Future of Alzheimer's Disease Research," July 26, 2007. www.news-medical.net/news/2007/07/26/28073.aspx.

Glossary

acetylcholine: A neurotransmitter that helps the brain form memories.

acetylcholinesterase: An enzyme that breaks down acetylcholine.

alpha-secretase: An enzyme that snips amyloid precursor protein in such a way that it cannot release beta-amyloid.

amyloid plaque: An abnormal clump of beta-amyloid protein that builds up between neurons in people with Alzheimer's disease.

amyloid precursor protein (APP): A larger protein that can be enzymatically snipped to form beta-amyloid.

apolipoprotein E (APOE) gene: A gene that comes in several forms, one of which is associated with an increased risk for Alzheimer's disease.

atrophy: Shrinkage.

autosomal dominant: Enabling a person to inherit a genetic mutation from only one parent in order to develop a disease.

axon: Part of a neuron through which chemical messengers and other materials are transported.

beta-amyloid: Small protein pieces that clump together to form plaques in the brains of people with AD.

beta-secretase: One of two enzymes that snip amyloid precursor protein in such a way that beta-amyloid is released.

cerebrospinal fluid (CSF): A liquid that surrounds the brain and spinal cord.

cholinesterase inhibitor: A drug that stops or slows down acetylcholinesterase in order to prevent it from interfering with communication between neurons.

chromosomes: Strings of genes that are coiled up into packages inside cells.

clinical trial: A study that takes place under controlled conditions.

computed tomography (CT): A type of imaging study that puts together X-rays from many different angles to form a cross-sectional image.

dementia: Condition in which the brain's ability to function is impaired to the point that it interferes with daily life.

dendrite: A thin branch of a neuron that receives chemical messages.

entorhinal cortex: A brain area involved with memory.

enzyme: A protein that speeds up or enables a specific chemical reaction.

epidemiologic study: A study of disease patterns based on observations of factors in people's everyday lives.

free radicals: Oxygen and nitrogen molecules that combine readily with other molecules.

gamma-secretase: One of two enzymes that snip amyloid precursor protein in such a way that beta-amyloid is released.

geriatrician: A physician who specializes in the health care and diseases of the elderly.

glutamate: A neurotransmitter involved with memory.

hippocampus: A brain area involved with learning and converting short-term memories into long-term memories.

inflammation: An immune system reaction to infection or injury.

lesion: An abnormal change in tissue.

magnetic resonance imaging (MRI): A type of imaging study that uses a magnetic field and sound waves to create a computerized image.

memantine: A drug that protects neurons by preventing too much glutamate from entering neuron receptors.

mild cognitive impairment (MCI): A condition in which people have greater memory problems than are normal for their age but not as severe as the memory problems of people with dementia.

mutation: A permanent change in a gene.

neurodegenerative: Causing brain tissue to deteriorate over time.

neurofibrillary tangle: A lesion made of abnormal, twisted threads of tau protein that forms inside neurons in people with Alzheimer's disease.

neuron: A nerve cell.

neuropsychological testing: Tests of different cognitive abilities, including memory, language, and problem solving.

neurotransmitter: Chemical messenger that delivers signals from one neuron to another.

oligomer: A small accumulation of up to a dozen beta-amyloid peptides stuck together.

peptide: A small section of a larger protein.

positron emission tomography (PET): A type of imaging study that detects radiation inside the body and translates it into a computerized image.

sundowning: Increased agitation in the late afternoon or evening.

synapse: The gap between neurons.

tau: A protein that binds to a neuron's transport tubes to keep them stable.

vascular dementia: A neurodegenerative disease caused by decreased blood flow to the brain.

ventricle: A fluid-filled space between brain areas.

Organizations to Contact

Alzheimer's Association

225 N. Michigan Ave., Fl. 17
Chicago, IL 60601-7633
Toll-Free 24/7 helpline: (800) 272-3900
Phone: (312) 335-8700
Toll-Free Fax: (866) 699-1246
E-mail: info@alz.org
Website: http://alz.org

This global organization provides funding for research and support and education to those affected by Alzheimer's disease. The website contains detailed information about the disease and living with the disease, downloadable publications, and other resources for patients and caregivers.

Alzheimer's Disease Education and Referral (ADEAR) Center

PO Box 8250
Silver Spring, MD 20907-8250
Toll-Free Phone: (800) 438-4380
Fax: (301) 495-3334
E-mail: adear@nia.nih.gov
Website: www.nia.nih.gov/Alzheimers

The center is operated by the National Institute on Aging as a comprehensive source of information about Alzheimer's disease. Its information specialists answer questions, provide publications, and refer people to other sources if necessary. Publications can also be downloaded from the website.

Alzheimer's Disease International (ADI)

64 Great Suffolk St.
London SE1 0BL
United Kingdom
Phone: +44 20 79810880
Fax: +44 20 79282357
E-mail: info@alz.co.uk
Website: www.alz.co.uk

This organization works to establish and strengthen Alzheimer's organizations around the world and to raise awareness about Alzheimer's disease and other dementias. The website contains information about the disease, help for people who have Alzheimer's disease and for their caregivers, and downloadable publications.

National Institute on Aging (NIA)

Bldg. 31, Rm. 5C27
31 Center Dr., MSC 2292
Bethesda, MD 20892
Phone: (301) 496-1752; Toll-Free: (800) 222-4225
Fax: (301) 496-1072
Website: www.nia.nih.gov

One of the National Institutes of Health, this agency supports and conducts research related to aging, trains scientists, and provides information. It leads the federal effort on Alzheimer's disease research. The website includes many downloadable publications and information on numerous studies.

For More Information

Books

Charles Atkins. *The Alzheimer's Answer Book: Professional Answers to More than 250 Questions About Alzheimer's and Dementia.* Naperville, IL: Sourcebooks, 2008. Easy-to-understand answers to questions about many aspects of Alzheimer's disease, including causes, prevention, diagnosis, treatment, and caregiving.

The Healing Project. *Voices of Alzheimer's: The Healing Companion; Stories for Courage, Comfort, and Strength.* New York: LaChance, 2007. A collection of first-person essays written by Alzheimer's patients, family members, and caregivers.

Barry R. Petersen. *Jan's Story: Love Lost to the Long Goodbye of Alzheimer's.* Lake Forest, CA: Behler, 2010. The author's memoir about the devastating impact of his wife's early-onset Alzheimer's disease.

Nancy L. Mace and Peter V. Rabins. *The 36-Hour Day: A Family Guide to Caring for People with Alzheimer Disease, Other Dementias, and Memory Loss in Later Life.* 4th ed. Baltimore: Johns Hopkins University Press, 2006. This invaluable guide written to help families cope with Alzheimer's disease includes many real-life examples.

Internet Sources

R. Morgan Griffin. "What It's Like to Have Dementia." WebMD, April 22, 2009. www.webmd.com/brain/features/understanding-dementia-symptoms.

Kirk Johnson. "More with Dementia Wander from Home." *New York Times*, May 4, 2010. www.nytimes.com/2010/05/05/us/05search.html.

Mary Brophy Marcus. "Husband and Wife Cope with Alzheimer's Progression." *USA Today*, April 5, 2010. www.usatoday.com/news/health/2010-04-05-blackwells05_ST_N.htm.

Jennifer Meyer. "Disappearing Act." *Oregon Quarterly*, Summer 2010. www.oregonquarterly.com/summer2010/feature4.php.

New York Times. "Many Alzheimer's Patients Find Comfort in Books." April 22, 2010. http://newoldage.blogs.nytimes.com/2010/04/22/many-alzheimers-patients-find-comfort-in-books/.

Websites

The Alzheimer's Research Forum (www.alzforum.org). A scientific community that provides the latest news, research databases, discussion forums, and interviews on the disease.

HBO: The Alzheimer's Project (www.hbo.com/alzheimers). This site features a four-part documentary and fifteen short films about many aspects of Alzheimer's disease.

KnowItAlz (www.knowitalz.com). An online community of Alzheimer's caregivers. Includes information, resources, and a blog to help caregivers look on the bright side.

Mayo Clinic (www.mayoclinic.com/health/alzheimers-disease/DS00161). The Alzheimer's section of this world-renown medical center's website contains detailed information about the disease, multimedia resources, expert answers to questions, and expert's blog.

WebMD Alzheimer's Disease Health Center (www.webmd.com/alzheimers). This site includes information, news, and videos about Alzheimer's disease.

Index

Picture Credits

About the Author

Jacqueline Adams is the author of forty books and more than a hundred magazine articles and stories for young readers. *Alzheimer's Disease* is her third title for Lucent Books, after *Steroids* and *Obsessive-Compulsive Disorder*. Her work won the *Highlights for Children* Fiction Contest in both 2003 and 2005 and the Society of Children's Books Writers and Illustrators Magazine Merit Award for Nonfiction in 2004.

Adams lives in western Pennsylvania, where she enjoys hiking and camping with her husband, son, and daughter; running with her dogs; and relaxing with her cats.